ANNIE HARLAND CREEK

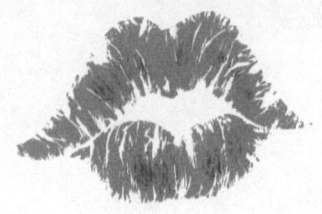

EVERNIGHT PUBLISHING ®

www.evernightpublishing.com

ANNIE HARLAND CREEK

ACKNOWLEDGEMENTS

To my family, friends and readers. Your belief in me is empowering. I am blessed to have you in my life. Thank you, once again, to Kerry for being the best beta reader on the planet.

There are no words to describe the gratitude I have for the team at Evernight publishing for continuing to support me in my writing journey. Last year, when Evernight accepted my first book, Kiss of Death, it was a dream come true. Now, with book three in print and book four almost finished, I can hardly believe I've come so far in such a short time. A big thank you to Stacey for her faith in me, Audrey for editing my work and for her helpful advice on how to swear in American LOL and, of course, Jay for her wonderful covers.

Evernight isn't just a publishing house. Once they accept you as an author, you become part of a family. The talented group of authors are a constant source of encouragement, support, and friendship. I hope that, one day, I can be as talented and successful as them.

ANNIE HARLAND CREEK

TAKE BACK THE NIGHT

Blood Brothers, 3

Annie Harland Creek

Copyright © 2018

Chapter One

Thunder rattled the windows of the room, waking the young woman from her fitful sleep. Her eyes flew open and widened in fear. She scanned the room as her heart thumped against the wall of her chest, robbing her of breath. *Where am I?* She drew her knees up under her chin, the soles of her feet brushing soft linen sheets. Her body sank into soft mattress and she leaned back against fluffy pillows as the realization hit her. *Not in a basement, that's for sure.* She let out an audible sigh but her heart refused to change its erratic pace. Her fingers brushed the scars along her neck. Scars not quite healed but faded none-the-less. No longer angry-looking red welts, the silvery white marks could easily be covered by makeup, if she chose to wear any. That wasn't going to happen any time soon.

A flash of lightning illuminated the room and her

memory returned. No, not a basement, but not her home either. She would never return to her home. Never. Evil knew where she lived. She hugged her knees tightly to her chest and shuddered as an image filtered through a crack in her carefully erected mental blocks. A hideous monster with long, yellowing nails and fangs. His skin drawn tight over his bony features, attracting attention to flaming red eyes that burned into her memory despite the hours of therapy. Laughing eyes that danced with delight at every scream he tore from her throat. Trembling, she closed her eyes and rested her forehead on her knees. Yes, Torke was evil but it was in his nature ... he was a monster. A real-life monster. It was the other man who taught her a valuable lesson. A lesson she would remind herself every day. Evil came in all shapes and forms. The ugly *and* the beautiful. Even handsome men with sparkling green eyes and disarming smiles had secrets. Some could hide a nature too despicable to fathom. *And if you have any sense, Susie Lister, you'll remember that!*

****

Terry Palmer gazed out of his office window, admiring the harbor. *Nice view.* Definitely a step up from his old, stuffy, windowless office. He opened the window, breathed in the fresh ocean air, and shuddered. *Well, almost fresh.* He crinkled his nose at the pungent smell of fish wafting up from the fishing boats as they unloaded their catch. Closing the window, he surveyed the room. *Not too shabby.*

Before leaving for her honeymoon, Meaghan had equipped his office with more computer equipment than he would ever need. Hell, he hardly knew what most of it was for. Despite being the commanding officer, his old office at the precinct had the bare minimum and he had managed just fine. *Humph. Probably Corel's influence.* He shook his head. *Goddamned David, sweeping in with his superpowers and sophistication.* What chance did a poor shmuck like him have to win Meaghan's affections when compared to Corel's charm? *What's done is done.* Better make the best of a bad situation. He'd accepted their job offer and he'd be damned if he didn't prove his worth.

An hour passed while he sat at his desk, staring through his open door at the reception area. *Come on, people. Where the hell are the clients?* If he wasn't being paid a salary, he'd be questioning his decision to leave law enforcement for private investigation. When the door buzzer sounded, he almost jumped out of his seat with enthusiasm. *Stay calm, Palmer. Don't look too anxious.* He kept his butt firmly planted in his seat and remained at his desk until the door had fully opened and the client had, hesitantly, made her way toward his office. Only then did he rise and move to offer his hand.

"Good morning Miss…?"

"Mrs. Whittaker. Janice Whittaker."

She accepted his hand but her eyes remained trained on the floor and Terry could feel the tremble in her clammy grasp as clearly as he could hear it in her voice. *Battered wife, maybe?*

"Nice to meet you, Mrs. Whittaker. I'm Terry Palmer." He motioned for her to sit on the upholstered chair beside his desk and offered her a coffee, which she declined. "What can we do for you?"

Janice Whittaker took a deep breath, then another before bursting into tears. Terry passed her a box of tissues but refrained from pressing her for an explanation. Years of experience taught him that it was better to allow the victim time to compose themselves and, at the moment, he had plenty to spare.

"I'm sorry." She sobbed into the tissue. "I just didn't know where to turn."

"You came to the right place," he told her. "Now, take your time and tell me who has upset you."

Janice nodded, blew her nose, and stared at him with bloodshot eyes. "It's my husband."

Terry nodded. "He beats you?"

"No, never. At least I used to believe that. Now…" She shook her head. "He's changed, Mr. Palmer. He ignores me and our children. He barely eats or sleeps. He stopped turning up for work at the factory and they sacked him, but he disappears for hours at a time and I have no idea where he's going."

"He may just be looking for work," Terry offered. "It's tough coming to terms with unemployment. Maybe—"

"He gets phone calls, all hours of the day and night. If I answer, the caller hangs up."

"So, you believe he's having an affair?"

"I don't know what to think." Janice leaned forward, covering her face with her palms. "Whoever calls him couldn't be making him happy. He gets agitated on the phone and then, he … I don't know … zones out."

Terry leaned back in his chair and linked his fingers behind his head. "Zones out?"

As she removed her hands from her face, Terry noticed the woman's pale complexion and the dark circles that lined her otherwise pretty eyes. Eyes filled with pain. He adjusted his position and leaned forward. "I'm sorry, Janice. I didn't mean to sound disrespectful. Could you please elaborate? It might give me more of an idea of how to help you."

Janice nodded but her shoulders dropped and she lowered her chin as she took another deep breath. "It's hard to explain." Her eyebrows knit and her mouth twisted into a grimace as she blurted, "It's like the other person is giving him instructions and he doesn't want to follow them. Then he just walks out of the house and doesn't come back for hours, sometimes days." She leaned forward and grabbed Terry's hands. "Please help me, Mr. Palmer. He isn't himself. I don't know where else to turn."

Terry removed his hands from the woman's grasp with as much sensitivity as a tough cop could muster. He wasn't comfortable with the physical contact. Not from a client. It didn't feel professional. There was an unwritten law in the force. Stay objective. Don't get personally involved. He saw no reason for private investigation to be any different, but he felt the sudden need to make her feel more comfortable, more at ease. He gave one of her hands a quick pat as he told her, "Please call me Terry. Now, I don't wish to offend you, but I must ask you some standard questions." He grabbed a pen from the desk and began scribbling on his notepad, ignoring the company-supplied laptop.

"Have you or your husband spoken to a doctor or counselor about this problem?"

"Six months ago, after his parents died in a car accident, Allan joined a support group at his doctor's suggestion. It seemed to helping, for a while."

Terry kept writing as he asked, "And this was before he started acting strangely?"

"Yes. He was depressed but he tried his best to cope. Life at home was a little *strained* but we managed."

"When did his behavior change?"

Janice tilted her head to one side, her gaze drifting to the ceiling. "About one month ago … no, six weeks, I think. He came home from a support meeting with a vague expression on his face and went straight to bed. The calls started the next day and every day since."

"Did you speak with his doctor?"

"She said she isn't allowed to discuss his

condition but assured me that he turns up to every meeting."

"Does he have any friends or family who he may confide in? A mutual friend?"

She shook her head. "He was an only child and his recent behavior has chased away all our friends. Even the neighbors give us the cold shoulder now."

Terry frowned. "Is he confrontational?"

Janice's eyes widened and she chewed on her bottom lip. "He just stares at them, at me and the kids. He either looks right through us as if we weren't there or else he glares like a madman. The neighbors won't even make eye contact with him anymore." She half-chuckled, half-cried. "Confrontational? He doesn't say a word. Not to me, not to anyone."

Terry tried to suppress a grin. "He speaks to someone, Janice. How else could he answer the mysterious caller?"

Janice crossed her arms over her chest and rubbed at the goosebumps that suddenly dotted her skin. "That's the creepiest part, Terry. He grunts … like an animal. He nods and grunts. It's like living in a horror movie with a madman. The kids are scared out of their wits."

"Could he be taking drugs?"

She shook her head. "If he is, I haven't seen any evidence and he hasn't taken any money out of our joint account. Do you think you can help us?"

Terry smiled as he handed her a standard client information form. "I'll do what I can. If you can give me his car registration number and a recent photo, I'll follow him for a few days and see where he goes, who he sees. Maybe that will give us some insight into his strange behavior. The address where he attends his meetings would be helpful too."

Janice looked up from the form. Color rose to her

cheeks and Terry anticipated her next question before she asked.

"Please don't tell my employer, Janice, but I forgot to tell you about the special promotion. As this is our first week, I was supposed to announce when you first walked in that, as our first customer, we will be waiving our fees."

Her hand went to her mouth and she sobbed. "Oh, my God. Thank you. Thank you so much. I wasn't sure how I was going to … oh, Terry, this means so much to me and the kids."

Terry felt the now-familiar tug as David intruded on his thoughts, the side effects of allowing the vampire to save his life.

"Promotion? Funny, I don't remember any promotion."

"She's desperate, Corel. Desperate and broke. I—"

"You did the right thing, Palmer. We're not in the business to make money from the needy. Give her all the assistance she needs."

"How's the honeymoon?"

"We're cutting it short. No, the romance isn't over. There's been a development."

"Damn you, Corel. Stop reading my mind. What's this development?"

"We'll discuss it when Meaghan and I return home."

"And that was all she wrote." Terry cursed under his breath. It infuriated him the way that Corel accessed his thoughts at will but cut the connection the moment things got interesting.

"Excuse me?"

He turned his attention back to Janice. "Sorry, I was just considering my next step." He took the completed form from her and, as she rose from her chair, shook her extended hand. "I'll give you a call the moment I have any information. Try and act as normal as possible around your husband but"—he handed her a business card—"if you ever feel threatened, call me immediately. Day or night."

She cupped her other hand, pressing her palms around his. "Thank you, Terry. I feel much safer knowing we have you looking after us."

Terry watched her leave and knew his thoughts should be focused on Janice and her children, but something else had his attention. What was so important that David would cut short his honeymoon?

Chapter Two

The forty-something psychologist looked up from her notes, her round, mocha-toned face expressionless as she asked, "So, Susie. How have you been sleeping lately? Is the medication helping?"

Susie removed her fingers from her mouth and hid her hands in her lap, hoping the doctor wouldn't see that her once manicured nails had been chewed to the quick. She shrugged her shoulders and sighed. "I guess they're helping. I only wake up once or twice a night lately."

"Are you back at work yet?" Dr. Dubois asked as she typed notes on her laptop.

Back to work? Susie broke out in a cold sweat. How could she go back to work at the gym? So many people … strangers. So many men with charming smiles hiding evil intent. Besides Anna and Dr. Dubois, she could barely speak to anyone, even Derrick, Anna's husband. Poor Derrick. He'd saved her life and given her the protection of a room in his house and she'd barely said two words to him since she'd taken up residence in his home. If only she could forget what he was, what Anna had also become.

"Susie?"

"Oh, I'm sorry. What was the question?"

"Have you gone back to work at the gym?"

"No. Not yet. I'm not…" She paused to catch her breath as her heart rate increased. "I'm not ready yet."

"Mmm." Dr. Dubois made another note. "I think it's time you joined my group counseling sessions. You need to interact with others, people who share your concerns. You'd be surprised how many have the same problem as you."

Susie almost laughed out loud. The same problem? How many of the patients in this group had been attacked by a coven of vampires? Who else had been kidnapped and chained to a wall for weeks while monsters fed on their blood? How many had blind dates turn out to be power-hungry maniacs who were willing to sacrifice innocent lives to get what they wanted?

"I know what you're thinking," the doctor told her.

"I seriously doubt that."

"This is a big step, but I truly believe that mixing with others and sharing your feelings will speed up your recovery process. Will you at least give it a try?"

Subconsciously, her fingers dove back into her mouth as she fought back the threatening tears. *Not ready. Don't want to*. Her thoughts turned to Anna and Derrick. She lived in their home, ate their food while she repaid them by forcing them to put up with her hysterical night terrors. She owed it to them to at least try. Nodding her head, she agreed.

"Okay, I'll try."

****

During the drive home, Susie sensed Anna's apprehension. Her best friend sat quietly behind the wheel of the BMW but Susie could tell that there were burning questions she needed answers to. If only she could find the words to ease her friend's pain.

"Doc Dubois wants me to join a group session," she finally shared.

"That's great," Anna replied with a smile in her voice that matched the one on her face. "How do you feel about that?"

"You sound like my shrink." Susie giggled for the first time since the incident.

"I've missed hearing that giggle," Anna told her

as she reached out to pat her friend's hand.

Instinctively, Susie reacted to Anna's freezing body temperature with a shudder as she pulled away. It broke her heart to see the sting of rejection on her friend's face.

"I'm sorry. That was rude of me. It's just—"

"I understand. Really, I do." Anna stared ahead at the road but her shoulders slumped and her eyes lost a little of their sparkle. "So, are you going to join the sessions?"

"I told the doctor that I would, but now I'm not so sure. I don't think I can face other people, not yet, and they're held during the day so you wouldn't be able to drive me. I'm nervous to drive while on the anti-depressant medication the doctor gave me."

"I'll arrange a driver to take you to and from your sessions. A female driver."

"You and Derrick have done enough for me already. I can't keep imposing like this."

"If it wasn't for me, you wouldn't have been in harm's way."

"*You* tried to convince me to cancel the blind date. I should have listened."

"We both know that you were a pawn. Torke used my ex to kidnap you so he could get to me. If I had just left town after Dad's funeral, you wouldn't have been caught up in all this."

"If you'd left town, I wouldn't have a best friend and you wouldn't have married that gorgeous millionaire of yours."

Anna grinned. "Yeah, there is that. So. No arguments. You're going to group counseling, you're going to get better, and there will be no more talk of being an imposition. Got it?"

"Yes, ma'am." She forced a smile but her heart

flopped in her chest. *Lord, give me the strength to get through this.*

****

As they entered the mansion and made their way to the living room, Susie noticed Derrick was not alone on the couch. Anna rushed to the gorgeous couple, giving them each a big hug as they rose to their feet.

"When did you guys get home? Wait a minute. You weren't due back for weeks."

"Something came up," David informed her, turning his head to smile at Susie. "We can talk about it later."

Message received, loud and clear. Don't upset the crazy lady. Susie knew it wasn't meant to be disrespectful, more to spare her feelings. Besides, if there was another monster loose on the streets, she'd rather not know about it. Her fragile nerves couldn't take any more. She decided to give them the opportunity to have their conversation in private.

"If you guys don't mind, I'm feeling a bit tired so I'm going to my room. Nice to have you back, Meaghan and David." She didn't wait for a reply, simply turning on her heels and hurrying away from the two newlywed couples. People who had found love despite the fact that all four were actually dead. *Or was it undead? Whatever. Their* nights were filled with lovemaking and staring into each other's eyes while hers were filled with night terrors and memories of agonizing torture. She longed for someone to share her troubles with. Someone who would not feel guilty and blame themselves the way Anna did. Someone who would not believe her to be crazy if she trusted them enough to tell the real story of how she ended up in the hospital needing a blood transfusion. The hospital staff immediately called for a psych assessment after Derrick's mind control had worn off and she remembered how she came to end up in the emergency room.

She shook the idea from her head, changed into her PJs, and climbed into her bed, pulling the covers up to her neck. Even if she somehow managed to find a man who believed her, how could she trust *him*? As much as she cared for Anna and her family, she could not forget what they were and how they survived on blood. What if something happened to turn them feral? If she couldn't trust them, how could she ever learn to trust a stranger?

Chapter Three

"Okay, spill."

Terry pushed his way past David and stood in the foyer of the mansion, trying to look unimpressed. When Meaghan had lived there undercover, she'd told him how extensive the grounds and property were, but hadn't come close to describing the grandeur. *So, this is how the other half lives?*

"Nice to see you too, Palmer. Why don't you come in?"

"Yeah, yeah, whatever." He did a quick perusal of the foyer and turned his attention back to his employer. "You asked me to come straight over. Don't keep me in suspense."

David gestured toward the living room. "Meaghan and the others are waiting inside."

"After you." Terry gestured back, hoping to get a better look at the house while walking behind the host.

"You're more than welcome to look around, Palmer, *after* I fill you in on my news."

Fuck! Terry growled under his breath. "Will you stay out of my head?"

"Probably not." David slapped his back. "So, you'd better get used to it."

"Terry!"

Meaghan flew at him with open arms. "It's so good to see you."

He hugged her back, apparently a little too long for her husband's liking because he suddenly felt a sharp pain in his head. Smiling at Meaghan, he lifted his finger behind her back, flipping David the bird.

"Nice to see you boys getting along so well," said

the young woman on the couch who Terry recognized as Anna, Derrick's wife. The pretty, copper-haired woman reached out and handed him a wineglass filled with red liquid. He sniffed the contents suspiciously.

"Oh for goodness sake, it's only wine," Meaghan informed him with a shake of her head. "Will you please take a break from being a detective and just enjoy an evening out with friends?"

Friends? He barely knew Anna and Derrick and, as for David … the guy may have saved his life but that hardly made him a friend. He'd stolen Meaghan's heart, something Terry had never been able to accomplish despite their long history together. He sat in the nearest seat, not only for convenience, but because it gave him a clear view of his new *friends* and allowed him to watch all exits, just in case he needed to find a quick escape. After another sniff to confirm that the drink was indeed wine and not blood, he took a sip and grunted. *Pretty good.*

"Okay, so what's this big news that cut short your honeymoon?"

"Anna had another premonition. She sensed evil heading this way on a larger scale than we've ever seen."

"Is that all?" Terry scoffed. "I've been on the force long enough to know there's always been evil around here. What are we talking about? Ten, Twenty? Thir—"

"Hundreds," Anna interrupted. "Maybe thousands will be affected."

"Shit!" Terry shook his head and noticed Derrick's stern expression. "Sorry, ladies." He turned to Anna. "I wasn't expecting those numbers. Are you sure?"

Anna sighed and shrugged her shoulders. "I can never be sure of my premonitions. Circumstances changes, fate intervenes. All I know for sure is that someone is planning a mass infection. Someone with an axe to grind. I feel what the person is doing is very personal. Revenge is the word that keeps popping into my head at the worst possible moments."

She turned her head toward her husband, grinned, and then dropped her chin a little when he winked. "Things are going to happen soon and fast. I feel it in my bones. Once it begins, the epidemic will gain momentum until we're overrun."

Terry gulped down his glass of wine, frowning as he passed it to David for a refill. "Epidemic? Don't you think that's a little melodramatic? I mean, you guys are all vampires. Can't you stop it?"

Anna shook her head but it was her husband who answered.

"Why do you think we called David and Meaghan back from their honeymoon? We've sent out an SOS to other covens. This is going to be big, Palmer. Bigger than we can handle on our own. A damn apocalypse."

"Apocalypse?"

Terry turned toward the startled female voice and his heart missed a beat. He hadn't seen the beautiful blonde since he'd first accepted the job working for David. If truth be told, she was part of the reason he'd taken the offer, hoping to run into her again. He'd thought her timid then but now, shaking in her pink pajamas and fluffy slippers, she looked positively terrified. Her voice trembled as she repeated her question.

"Did you say apocalypse?" Her eyes glazed over and her already pale face turned a shade lighter. He rushed to her, catching her as her legs buckled, and helped her to the seat he had vacated. She nodded a thank you but remained silent as Anna asked if she remembered him from the office.

"Yes. I remember," she answered in a voice

almost too quiet to perceive. "I'm sorry to have interrupted but … I just came out to get a glass of water from the kitchen and heard parts of your conversation."

"You're perfectly safe here, Susie," David told her. "We won't let anything happen to you."

"You can't protect me during the day," she reminded him. Suddenly, she turned to Terry then back to David. "I mean…"

"It's all right, Susie. Terry knows what we are."

"Oh," she replied before her middle two fingers disappeared into her mouth. When her chin dropped, Terry suspected she would likely remain silent for the rest of the conversation. As a detective, he'd seen victims of abuse retreat into their own thoughts. She was shutting them all out and he couldn't blame her. David had explained how she had been kidnapped and tortured by vampires. Now she had this to deal with. *Poor little mouse.*

****

Calm, blue ocean, calm, blue ocean. Susie repeated the mantra taught to her by her doctor, but the other word, the latest horror, kept intruding into her thoughts. *Apocalypse.* The end of the world. She wanted to get up from the chair and return to her room, her sanctuary, but her legs refused to cooperate. Mr. Palmer, who had been kind enough to prevent her from face planting, now crouched on the floor beside her. *Too close.* She wished he would move away. Far away. Far enough that she wouldn't smell his cologne, the same cologne worn by Patrick, her blind date. The monster who'd kidnapped and ransomed her for a chance at eternal life. *No, Susie. He can't hurt you anymore. David killed him.* She reminded herself. The truth made no difference. The memories remained, and although Terry Palmer seemed to be a lovely man, he was still too close for comfort. When she leaned away in her seat, his head snapped up and he rose to his feet to find a chair at the opposite side of the room. She sighed, realizing that she had been holding her breath and waited for the conversation to resume.

Terry spoke first. "All right, let's say I believe you. Does that mean I should be looking for people with strange-looking skin conditions or coughing up blood?"

She noticed he winced when he looked in her direction, as if he expected her to faint. She threw her shoulders back and tried to look unaffected by his statement. All eyes turned to her and her heart sank. *Have I really become that pathetic? Will the confident, happy Susie ever show her face again?*

"I'm not sure," Anna answered. "I feel that at the beginning of the disease there will only be subtle changes. Personality changes. Black magic is devious. It sneaks up on the victim. Nothing in my premonitions suggests physical transformations. Not until the very end."

"That's not much to go on." Terry scratched his head and Susie felt a pang of pity for him. Azure Waters was a big town and he would be working the case alone during the day. How could he cover such a big area on his own? He wouldn't be able to tell his police buddies that black magic was involved as that would expose him to ridicule. Her heart went out to him.

"I'll keep my ear to the ground while I tail my client's husband," he told the group as he rose from his seat, checking his watch. "Damn, I'm already late getting to his house."

Susie nodded her goodbye as he bid her good night. He turned to walk with David to the front door. The cotton shirt he wore strained across his broad shoulders, tapering down to a narrow waist and hips that swayed a little when he walked. He had a confident stride. Almost a swagger. This man had seen evil in many forms and yet, rather than cower from it, he faced it head-on. She envied his conviction, his passion to save the world. A world that now terrified her.

Chapter Four

As he gulped down the last drop of his coffee, Terry noticed movement at the front door of the house across the street from where he had parked. *Here we go.* He checked his watch. *About fucking time.* He placed his empty thermos in the cup holder of his company car—another perk of the job—and pushed the starter button on the dashboard of the SUV while he waited for the suspect to back out of his driveway. The man appeared to be in no hurry.

"Come on, come on. Get with the program." Terry moaned, becoming increasingly agitated as the car slowly reversed onto the street. He'd barely slept the previous night during the stakeout and the thought of following at a snail's pace added to his annoyance. How old was this guy? Ninety?

Keeping at a safe distance, he followed the car out of the palm tree-lined, suburban street and into town where he parked half a dozen car spaces behind when the suspect pulled over. He waited until Mr. Whittaker alighted his vehicle and entered a red brick building before he left his own car and followed. The sign on the door was nondescript, only the number and street name. Terry made a note in his iPhone before entering. Inside, signage by the elevator informed him that this was a professional building used by medical people, two psychologists, a dermatologist, an immunologist, an addiction psychiatrist, and a cardiologist. Half the building remained unused, the rooms for advertised for lease. He struck three of the professions from his mental list. As far as Janice Whittaker had told him, her husband had no history of heart or allergy problems. That left the head-shrinkers. Addiction psychiatrist? *Hmmm. Maybe Allan has been able to conceal a drug addiction after all. Third floor it is.* He pressed the "up" arrow and waited for the elevator, tapping his foot impatiently on the tiled floor.

Unexpectedly, the loud clap of his inexpensive leather sole hitting the vinyl was joined by a rhythmic pit-pat of heels as they came up behind him. A timid, melodic voice greeted him.

"Hello, Mr. Palmer."

He turned to greet the most beautiful woman he'd ever met.

"Susie? I didn't expect to see you here." *Not that I'm complaining.* She was a sight for sore eyes and the main reason he'd lost sleep last night. He couldn't stop thinking about her. He tugged at the collar of his buttoned shirt and cleared his voice. "Did David send you?"

She lowered her chin and shook her head. "I have an appointment."

"I hope you're not ill." He considered the doctors on the notice board.

Her face flushed with color. "No, not ill. It's not really an appointment, I guess. I have a group session, I … look, Mr. Palmer. I'm don't want to sound rude but … I'm not comfortable talking about it."

Terry held up his hands, palms facing her. "Sorry. Once a cop, always a cop. I tend to ask a lot of questions."

The elevator doors opened and he motioned for her to enter ahead of him. She smiled. It wasn't much of a smile but enough to send a rush of blood to his cock. He wondered if there was a way to coax a bigger smile from those plump, bow-shaped lips. If there was, he'd make it a priority to find it. Something told him that it would be worth the effort.

"What floor?" he asked after pressing the third for himself.

"Fourth, please," she mumbled, staring at her shoes. She continued to gaze at her feet until they stopped at his floor. He reluctantly stepped out, holding the doors open with his hands as he asked if she would like a lift home after she finished her meeting.

"No thank you, Mr. Palmer. Anna has a car waiting for me."

"Terry. Please call me Terry," he reminded her, positive that he'd mentioned that at every one of their previous meetings. "I hope we run into each other again soon." He managed to get the words out before the doors shut, ending the conversation.

****

All right. Where the hell did you go? Unable to locate Allan Whittaker in the addiction specialist's room, he'd checked out all the rooms on Level Three without success. Could Allan be with the doctor? No. He'd been close behind, too close to lose him so quickly. The conversation with Susie had been short and sweet but not in the usual sense. Her answers had been short, yet there was a sweetness about her that intrigued him.

"Are you looking for the group session?" the gruff voice behind him asked, shocking him back to reality. *Not good, Palmer. Never let down your guard.* The elderly man beside the open office door struck what he appeared to believe was a menacing pose. He stood, hands on hips, glaring over a pair of horn-rimmed spectacles. Terry let out an audible sigh. *Damn it, man. How can you be so careless as to attract attention?*

"Yes. The group session. I forgot where it was being held." He smiled as he lied through his teeth, hoping that he could charm his way out of the situation.

"One floor up," snapped the man, obviously

annoyed to have been interrupted. "Third room on the left."

"Much obliged." Terry nodded in thanks as he beat a hasty retreat to the elevator. *Geez. That* guy needed group therapy or possibly anger management classes. *So, fourth floor it is.* At least he may get the opportunity of running into Susie. Another glimpse of her would improve his afternoon.

Following asswipe's instructions, he got off at the next floor and turned left, making his way down the corridor. The third room had its chairs arranged in a circle. Fifteen butts occupied seats. *Big group.* A bespectacled dark-skinned woman who looked to be in her mid-forties sat with a notebook on her lap, facing sideways to him. He kept out of her line of vision, peering through an opening in the door. *Aha.* Allan Whittaker sat bolt upright, staring straight ahead while a petite, elderly woman with silver hair talked about her encounter with a mugger. Whatever had Allan's attention had nothing to do with the old lady. There was no reaction at all from him, even when she burst into tears. While the others in the group all offered their sympathies, he remained stony-faced and emotionless. *What's going on in that brain?* The screech of chair legs on the wooden floor made him shudder and he turned in the direction of the sound. A blonde woman, who had her back to Terry, offered the sobbing lady a box of tissues. The bounce of her golden locks made his heart thud against the wall of his chest. *Susie?*

****

Susie extended the tissues to the sobbing woman. She wanted to offer words of encouragement, words of hope to the frail, little woman, but she had none. Evil thrived in this town. More evil than dear old Mrs. Short could comprehend. If the elderly lady was lucky, the mugging would be the worst thing that ever happened to her. If not? Susie closed her eyes tight and sent up a silent prayer. *Let this be the worst thing.*

A lump formed in her throat, threatening to choke her, or, at the very least, steal her voice. She knew that Dr. Dubois expected her to share her feelings with the group, discuss her own reason for attending therapy. How could she? No one would believe her. She'd be locked away in a nuthouse. The story she'd fabricated for the doctor was nothing compared to the horror of the weeks she'd suffered, chained in the abandoned warehouse. She'd lied, saying that the trauma of being kidnapped had caused her mind to shut down, block out most of what had happened. If only that were true. She remembered every detail. Every bite to her flesh. Every threat to her body. A shudder ran through her and she dropped the box of tissues.

A hand reached down and passed her the box. She glanced up at the owner of the hand. A nice-looking man with milk chocolate-colored skin and dark eyes. She accepted the tissues, passed them to the woman, and quickly returned to her seat, diverting her eyes to the opposite side of the room. Big mistake. The man facing her wore a blank, almost maniacal expression on his pale face. He seemed to be staring right through her, as though he couldn't even see her. Another shiver shook her, drawing the attention of the doctor.

"Are you all right, Susie?"

Susie nodded as she chewed on the skin of her fingertips, the nails too short now to bite.

"Would you like to share your story with the class?" Dr. Dubois asked, directing her question to Susie, who shook her head vehemently. "Perhaps next time?"

The doctor sighed, writing something in her notebook before asking another patient. "Allan. We haven't heard from you for a while. How have you been?"

The strange man with the dead, focused eyes remained eerily silent as he continued to stare into space. A few of the other attendees whispered among themselves until the doctor shushed them. "Does anyone have anything to share? Anyone at all?"

"I'm ready to share my story with the group," the dark-eyed man announced. His deep, honey-toned voice sounded smooth and confident. Odd for a situation like this. A room full of broken, hopeless people. A stillness came over the group, as if the richness of his speech commanded their full attention. Even odd Allan turned his head to listen.

"My name is Beau and my story begins many years ago. A man came to my small village. I recognized the danger, immediately. He'd come with the intention to stir up trouble and that, he did. He convinced my woman that I was no good for her and eventually turned the whole village against me. His actions drove me bankrupt. I lost everything. My woman, my friends and family, my home and my business. Forced to leave my home, I've attempted to make a new life here. At first, I felt overwhelmed, afraid. But now … now I see the beauty of your small town."

His piercing dark eyes bore through her as he emphasized the word *beauty*, and she felt a rush of blood to her cheeks before she looked away.

"I'm ready to begin a new life, here in Azure Waters. The man who ruined my life remains in my thoughts, but I know my future looks brighter. I will prevail." He flashed a toothy grin. "With the help of you wonderful people, of course."

The class applauded his courage and even Susie returned his beaming smile despite the nagging feeling in the pit of her stomach. His confident speech and determination almost sounded convincing. *Almost*. There was something in his words that didn't ring true. Perhaps he tried too hard to convince the doctor? Maybe, like her, his real story would sound too far-fetched to be believed? Whatever the case, she found it difficult to trust him. Another handsome man with a hidden agenda. *What are you hiding, Beau?*

****

Tempting as it was to wait outside the room for another opportunity to speak to Susie, Terry hurried back to the elevator the moment the session finished. *What a bust.* Allan barely opened his mouth, let alone divulged any useful information to help the case. If he hadn't turned his head to watch the big black guy speak, he would have appeared, for all intents and purposes, dead. His expressionless face didn't change for the entire hour that Terry had spent leaning against the wall, listening to stories of shattered dreams and tales of woe. Some cried, others shook their heads in sympathy. Allan Whittaker stared into space. He didn't even respond to the doctor when she asked if he had anything he wanted to share. Susie, he noticed, almost had a meltdown when the doctor asked her the same question. Beads of sweat dotted her forehead and even from where he stood, he could see her hands shaking in her lap as she shook her head vehemently. *Poor kid.*

From his car, he watched a procession of people exit the red brick building and head off in different directions. All except the big dude who waited by the door. Gut instinct told him that the guy was waiting for someone. A knot in his stomach told who. Susie. When she stepped out, the man spoke to her, catching her off-guard. She jumped back, her hand automatically covering her throat. It took every ounce of Terry's willpower to keep his butt planted on the driver's seat. *No real danger*, he reminded himself. *He's just a man attracted to a beautiful woman. Fuck!* He smacked the inside of the car door with the back of his hand. He should have waited for her outside the room. Now another guy had beaten him to the punch. A big, handsome, smooth-talking guy. *Fuck! Fuck! Fuck!*

****

"I'm sorry to have startled you," the man apologized. "I noticed you in the session and just wanted to introduce myself. My name is Beau."

Susie ignored the extended hand, keeping her eyes trained on her shoes as a rush of heat warmed her cheeks.

"Susie," she told him, hoping he would go away now he had her name.

"A pleasure to meet you, Susie." He held his hand out a few seconds longer before giving up and slipping it into his pocket. "What was your first impression of our group?"

Susie raised her chin and faced him as she pondered his statement. "How did you—"

"I would have remembered you if you'd been in the session before. I never forget a beautiful face."

Susie held tight to the strap of her handbag, fighting the temptation to draw her fingers to her mouth. To chew her bitten-down nails. As handsome as he was, this man's attention sent a shiver down her spine, and not in a good way. Tiny hairs on the back of her neck prickled and stood at attention. His smooth words might melt the hearts of other women, but they drove an ice stake into hers. She'd met his kind before. *Gotta get out of here.*

As if on cue, a black limousine pulled up to the curb and the female driver jumped from the car to open the passenger door. "Are you ready to leave, Miss

Lister?"

With a half-smile and a brief nod in Beau's direction, she hurried to the car, anxious to return to the mansion and avoid further eye contact with the smooth-talking stranger. Even with her back to him, she could sense him watching her as she scooted into her seat.

"I'll see you next week, Susie Lister," he called to her before the driver closed her door.

No, you won't, she decided as the car pulled away.

Chapter Five

Despite the knowledge that her friends slept upstairs, only a scream away, Susie feared the solitude as she waited for the sun to set. She shook her head and laughed at the irony of the situation. The darkness terrified her, but not as much as the fear of being alone, helpless. Until she'd accepted Anna's invitation to move into the mansion, sleep had eluded her. Even now, nightmares still woke her, but Anna and Derrick's home offered *some* protection from the things that went bump in the night. That was the promise, anyway.

At last, the final rays of sunlight began to disappear behind pink clouds. She followed her daily routine, closing all the block-out curtains in the kitchen, dining and living rooms. She switched on a few table lamps before the darkness crept over the room as she waited for her hosts to rise from their beds.

****

"But you were making progress," Anna protested after listening to Susie's decision. "You can't give up just because some guy hit on you."

Susie sat beside Anna on the couch, curling her feet under her bottom as she chewed on the smidgen of nail left on her right index finger. "I've been playing it over and over in my head while I waited to talk to you. There is something … *wrong* with that man."

Anna playfully slapped Susie's hand from her mouth. "Why? Because he told you that you're beautiful? I hate to tell you this, Susie, but you *are* beautiful"—she motioned to Susie's attire—"even in your cartoon pajamas and bed socks. He isn't the first to notice and he won't be the last."

Shaking her head, Susie argued, "No. It's more than that. He sends shivers down my spine."

Anna frowned. "Isn't that usually a good thing?"

"Isn't what usually a good thing?"

Susie turned toward Derrick, who'd entered from the kitchen. Between his fingers, he balanced three goblets by their stems in one hand and a bottle of Cabernet in the other. As he placed them all on the glass coffee table, she rose from her seat.

"If you'll excuse me, I'm off to bed."

Derrick's mouth tightened into a grimace as his eyebrows knit. "Aren't you going to stay and share a glass of wine with us?"

She shook her head but refused to look in his direction as she made her apology. "Sorry, I'm not feeling so great." As she rushed from the room, she called over her shoulder, "Have a good night."

When she reached her room at the front of the mansion, she stopped cold. Someone, or something, sat on her bed. She took a step back and prepared to scream when the familiar voice informed her, "It's me, Susie. It's only me."

"How did you...?" Susie turned her head right to left, then back to the bed. "Oh, geez, Anna. I don't think I'll ever get used to that."

Anna patted the bed. "Come and tell me what's really bothering you."

Before closing the door, Susie motioned to the overhead light and flipped the switch. "If you don't mind, some of us don't have night vision." She trudged over to the bed and plonked down beside her friend, as close as she could emotionally manage.

"Derrick still terrifies you, doesn't he?" Anna guessed.

"It's not him." Susie held her hands over her face

and shook her head. "I know he's a good man, it's just—"

"He's a vampire?"

Removing her hands from her face, Susie stared into Anna's eyes and confessed, "The vampire thing is a big part of it, but it's more than that." Her voice trailed off as she wondered how to explain without offending her best friend. "Look. I know deep down that Derrick wouldn't hurt me the same as I know that about David and Meaghan and—"

"And me?"

She nodded and averted her eyes.

"But you still fear us?"

"I fear everything!" she cried out, unable to prevent the words from escaping. Unable to close the flood gates on her despair. "I fear the dark. I can't stand to be in a room with a male. Every sound makes my heart beat like a war drum. Every shadow steals away the oxygen from my lungs. I'm frightened living here but terrified of moving out. I miss work but I couldn't deal with male clients while I feel this way. I hate imposing on you, eating your food, accepting your hospitality while contributing nothing. I…" The sob escaped, followed closely by a torrent of tears. She wiped at her nose with the back of her hand. Anna reached out to hug her but she withdrew, reluctant to be touched.

"It's okay, sweetie. Let it out."

"I'm tired of being afraid. I want to be happy again, Anna. Will that ever happen?"

"I can help you, if you'll let me."

Susie gasped, shaking her head vehemently. "I can't. I just can't do that."

"It would only be a small exchange of blood. You wouldn't even feel it. Then, I'll always be able to connect with you. Find you. Ease your mind."

"No!" She jumped from the bed, then turned her back to her friend, unable to face her. "I'm sorry, Anna. I know you're only trying to help me, but … I can still feel their mouths on my skin." She rubbed at the back of her neck as a wave of nausea rose in her stomach. "Their hands on my body. I can smell the blood on their breath. My blood. I just can't do it."

"It's okay. No one is going to force you to do anything. I promise."

Susie kept her back turned to her friend, partly wanting the protection of a blood link. The other part, the fragile part, suspected she would never again experience the warmth of someone's touch, human or otherwise.

"I'm really tired. If you don't mind, I think I'd like to go to sleep."

Anna rose from the bed. She raised her hand and reached out to touch Susie's shoulder, but when Susie flinched, she dropped it down by her side.

"Sweet dreams," she said as she opened the bedroom door. "If you get worried, we'll be right outside."

As Anna closed the door behind her, Susie leaned her forehead on the paneled wood and whispered, "That's part of the reason *why* I'm worried."

****

This must be the most boring man on the face of the earth.

Allan Whittaker had left the meeting, stopped in at the hardware store, and returned home without incident. He spoke to no one, even his wife who met him at the front door with a hug. While she hugged, he stood motionless. Expressionless. A cold fish. No. A fish at least put some energy into swimming around. This guy made a sloth look lively. As the front door closed behind the oddly matched couple, Terry decided to call it a day.

He stretched his arms out behind his head and yawned. Besides, he hadn't slept at all the night before and the funky smell under his armpit reminded him that he hadn't changed his clothes since the stakeout. A shower sounded pretty good about now. He pushed the ignition button and headed home.

****

Singing at the top of his voice in the shower, Terry paused. *Was that the phone?* He listened intently. *There it is again.* The familiar ring tone of his mobile. Wrapping a towel around his waist, he jumped from the recess and ran into the bedroom, shaking the water from his hair as he dug into his jeans pocket, locating the phone just as the caller hung up. *Fuck! Just when the day started off so great too.* After eight hours of uninterrupted sleep and a steaming hot shower, his thoughts had been focused on a big café breakfast, not receiving a six AM call. He checked the caller ID and scratched his damp head. *Why would the station be calling me?* With a shrug, he pushed the "call back" button as he sat down on the edge of the bed.

"Azure Waters' police department. Officer Stone speaking."

"Adam. It's Terry."

"Hey boss. I just tried calling you."

"I'm not your boss anymore, so Terry will do. What's up?"

"We had a murder last night. A woman was stabbed to death in her home. Thank God her kids were playing at a friend's house, but they made the grisly discovery when they came home for dinner. The father is missing but his prints are all over the murder weapons."

"Weapons?"

"Yeah"—Adam cleared his throat—"weapons as in plural. He used a machete and a knife. His bloody footprints are everywhere, Terry. I'm not exaggerating. Everywhere. I've never seen so much blood."

Terry steadied himself as the realization hit him. Still, he had to ask. Had to hope he was wrong. "What does this murder have to do with me?"

"The kids found what's left of their mother in her walk-in closet. She had a phone in one hand and a business card in the other. We think she was trying to call you. Possibly for help. The woman's name was Janice Whittaker. Did you know her personally?"

The droplets of water froze on his skin. "She is ... was, a client."

Despite years of hardening his heart against the horrific crime scenes of his previous occupation, Terry felt sick to his stomach. *I should have been there. I should have protected her.*

"Where is she, Adam?" he asked, grimacing at the tremble in his voice.

"She's in the morgue. We're waiting for interstate family members to identify the body."

"The kids?"

"Staying with children's services until the relatives arrive. I think they'll be in therapy for a while. A long, long while. How could someone do that to their own wife, knowing that the kids would discover the body?"

A man who's discovered that his wife is having him followed, that's who. "Any leads on the suspect?"

"None. It's like he disappeared off the face of the earth."

Terry took a deep breath and let it out slowly. "Okay. Thanks for letting me know, Adam. *I'll* head down to the morgue and identify the body. No point in putting the relatives through that too. I'll call into the station on the way back. I know you guys will have questions for me."

He hung up the phone without waiting for an answer. *Whittaker must have spotted me.* He closed his eyes and threaded his fingers through his still damp hair, digging the tips into his scalp before tugging at the roots. *I'm so sorry I let you down, Janice. So sorry.*

****

"Detective Palmer? What are you doing here? I mean … were you expected?"

"Damn." Terry palmed his forehead as he realized his mistake. "I'm sorry, Susie. I totally forgot that they wouldn't be about at this time of the day."

"Would you like me to give them a message?" the trembling woman asked between the crack in the chained door.

He suspected that she thought the chain would protect her from intruders, but he knew better. A solid kick would break it with ease. Not that he was about to inform her of that. She already looked as though she might faint.

"Nah." He waved his hand in the negative. "I'm having a bad morning is all and just wanted to talk to someone. Meaghan is usually my 'go to girl' for a sympathetic ear. I guess that's over now." With a shrug of his shoulders, he turned to leave.

"Wait!" the timid voice called to him. "I'm usually a good listener … that's if you want to talk about it with me?"

Terry paused. Meaghan had told him that Susie rarely spoke to anyone. It must have taken a great deal of courage to make that offer. How could he refuse?

"That would be great … as long as you're not busy."

She closed the door and unfastened the chain before opening it wide, although she cowered behind it.

"Please, come in. I'll put the coffee on."

As he made his way toward the kitchen, he glanced sideways at her oversized t-shirt and baggy tracksuit pants. They reminded him of the pajamas she'd worn the last time he had been to the mansion. A pale-blue scrunchie held her hair in a loose bun, drawing attention to her fresh, makeup-free complexion. Her bare feet pattered on the Italian tiles as she led him through the house. An untrained eye might assume she preferred this comfortable attire, but he'd seen this behavior before. Like the many female victims of abuse he'd interviewed over the years, she hid her curves beneath the loose-fitting clothes, hoping to lessen her appeal. *As if that is possible.* She would still look stunning, even if she wore a hessian potato sack. He wished he could tell her that without scaring her away.

He followed her through the large foyer, past the elegant lounge room, and into the biggest kitchen he'd ever laid eyes on.

"Holy crap! The Corels must entertain a lot if they need a kitchen this big."

Susie filled the jug with water from the sink, set the pot to brew, and collected two mugs from a cup holder. "No one, besides you, has been here since I arrived. Mind you, that could be *because* I'm here."

"Oh." *How do I respond?* None of the scenarios seemed like a good topic to mention. Either they thought that their guests might be tempted to eat her, or she would freak out having extra vampires in the house. *Keep your big mouth shut, Palmer.*

"Would you like a cookie with your coffee?" she asked as she poured their drinks.

Her question confounded him. "They keep food in the house?"

Susie laughed. It came bubbling from between her

lips in a sudden burst of bell-toned notes. The smile lit up her face and he knew it was a memory that would remain etched in his brain. *Beautiful.*

"They *can* eat. They just don't need to eat. I, on the other hand, do."

Terry lowered his chin and scratched the back of his neck. "Sorry, my brain isn't working this morning." *Especially after witnessing the loveliest smile I've ever seen.*

She motioned for him to sit at the kitchen table and carried over a tray with sugar, milk, and a plate of chocolate chip cookies. They looked great, but his stomach still hadn't settled from his visit to the morgue. Nevertheless, he took one and nibbled the dark chocolate jutting from the edge.

"You mentioned that you were having a bad morning. What can I do to help?"

Smile again. Another smile like that would certainly brighten his day. Instead, he hesitated. She'd experienced worse horrors than he'd ever known. His morning didn't compare to her past. *Walk on egg shells.*

"I lost a client today." *Hopefully she won't ask for details.*

"The case you spoke to David about? The married woman who thought that her husband was cheating?" She took the seat opposite him and kept her hands in her lap.

Damn. Now what? "Yeah, that's the one."

"What happened? Did she decide to go with another agency?"

Fuck, fuck, fuck. "Not exactly."

Susie took in a deep breath and let it out slowly. "I may not have Anna's psychic abilities or Meaghan's cop intuition, but I do have a good deal of common sense. They told you about me, didn't they? You're holding back information because you're afraid I'll shatter into a million pieces."

Terry's nose crinkled and his mouth twisted into a half-smile. "Am I really so transparent?"

"Crystal clear."

She flashed him another smile. A brief, beautiful, bewitching smile that almost reached her eyes. Almost.

"Now. Can we stop dancing around the truth?"

"Only if you call me Terry." *As if I haven't asked her a million times already.*

"Okay, Terry. Tell me what happened, and I want the truth this time."

He took a sip of his coffee and then a deep breath. What would he do if she lost it?

"My client was murdered last night."

Her hand shot to her mouth and her eyes widened in horror. *Idiot. Now look what you've done.*

"Do you know *who* murdered her?"

"It looks like it was her husband. Actually, I'm sure it was."

When her hand dropped back to the table, she seemed calmer. "Oh, that's good. No, of course it's not good, I mean … I'm glad it wasn't…"

He saved her the pain of naming the creature that he was told had ruined her life. "Nothing supernatural. Just a man."

****

Just a man? The words sent a shiver down her spine. *Just* a man? It was 'just a man' who lured her to the vampires' den. Just a man who bartered her like cattle in exchange for everlasting life. She reached for the coffee cup, but her trembling hand knocked over the sugar bowl, spilling the contents everywhere.

"I'm so clumsy these days." she told him as she swept the crystals with her hand onto an empty plate.

He reached out to help. Their fingers met and she

jumped at the contact, spilling more sugar on the table.

"I've upset you," he apologized with a puppy dog expression that caused her further embarrassment. "I shouldn't have told you about the murder."

She turned her head away, hoping it would be easier to explain if she didn't have to face him. Didn't lose herself in those emerald-green eyes. "I … I don't like to be touched."

"I'm sorry, Susie. I wasn't trying to—"

She turned to face him. "I know you didn't mean anything by it. I can't stand even Anna touching me and she's my best friend. It's something I'm trying to deal with. That's why I've started group sessions with Doctor Dubois."

Terry's reaction took her by surprise.

"Fuck!"

She frowned her disapproval at his curse word. "Excuse me?"

He shook his head. "Sorry. It just came out." He palmed his forehead before telling her, "I completely forgot that I saw you at the session."

Wow, that's not insulting at all. She opened her mouth to speak but he interrupted.

"Allan Whittaker. He's part of your group."

"Allan Whittaker?"

"You know … the strange guy who didn't say a word during the session."

Susie gasped. "I remember him. He barely moved. I don't remember him even blinking. He gave me the creeps."

"He's the murderer. He killed his wife and left the body for her kids to find."

She shuddered as she pictured the poor children beside the body of their dead mother. "Did they catch him?"

45

"No, not yet. Maybe it would be better if you skip group therapy for a while. At least until he's in custody."

Fine by me. I'm not keen on seeing Beau again anytime soon. But Anna would be disappointed if she didn't learn to reconnect with people. "I don't know. I really need those sessions. I doubt that he'd come back. He must know the police are looking for him."

"I'd feel better if you stayed away." He raised his hand, as though he might reach for her, then dropped it back in his lap.

"It's not like I enjoy being part of that group, Terry. Anna thinks it will help me if I can talk to someone about my experience. Someone who isn't a—"

"Vampire?"

With a shrug she added, "I can't live like this anymore. You probably won't believe it, but I used to be outgoing. Fun, even."

His mouth twisted a little at one corner in a half-smile but the green in his eyes brightened to a deeper shade of emerald. "If you like, you can always talk to me."

A kaleidoscope of butterflies took flight in her stomach. Fear? Excitement? She wasn't sure which. "I … I'll have to think about it," she told him. "Would that be okay?"

He rose from his seat. "Sure. Take your time. Whenever you're ready, I'm here for you."

Halfway to the front door, he turned. "I mean it, Susie. I'm here for you. Any time, day or night. I don't have superpowers, but I'm pretty handy with my fists and I'm a crack shot with a revolver."

Lifting his jacket aside, he showed her the handgun he had holstered in his belt before he reached into his top pocket and handed her a business card, keeping his fingers on the furthest edge to avoid touching her. As grateful as she was for his consideration, somehow it caused a pang of disappointment. She was still pondering her reaction as she watched his car travel down the long driveway and out of sight.

Chapter Six

You can do this. Susie marched into the kitchen knowing that all four of her hosts were in the room, drinking what she hoped was wine. They looked as though they had all stepped from the page of a fashion magazine. David, the cheekier brother, rocked a white t-shirt and navy-blue jeans. His dark hair matched his brother's but she noticed his eyes were a slightly deeper shade of blue. Derrick wore camel-colored chinos and a pale-blue buttoned shirt that matched his wife's floral cotton dress. Anna's copper curls had grown longer than when she and Susie had first met, although still not as long as Meaghan's waist-length, pale-blonde hair which had been tied back in a ponytail, making her look even younger than her years. Her tight jeans hugged her curves, as did her pink off-the-shoulder top. David's hand rested on Meaghan's bottom, his fingers splayed to cover most of her butt cheek.

Mid-conversation, they stopped and turned to face her. She suspected she'd surprised them, considering she rarely found the courage to be in a room with both couples at the same time. Too many vampires. Too many memories.

Meaghan held out a glass. "Susie. Join us for a glass of merlot."

"Thanks." She accepted the drink with a smile as she tried to control the trembling in her hand. *They won't hurt you. You know that. Relax.*

"I heard you had a visit from Palmer today," David informed her as, holding his wife's hand, he led the group into the living room. "I hope he didn't distress you."

Susie closed her eyes and grimaced. *Am I really that pathetic? Have I changed that much?* "No. He didn't upset me. He was very pleasant, very considerate."

The brothers exchanged knowing looks. *What were they saying to each other?* She knew they had a telepathic link, a blood connection. She also knew that David was able to connect with Terry through a similar connection. Were they discussing *her* or Terry Palmer?

Once in the room, they separated into couples. Meaghan and David curled up on one couch while Anna and Derrick snuggled in the other. Susie plonked herself into one of the single seats and resisted the urge to chew her fingers. *Be brave. You've got this.*

"I'd like to ask you all for advice, if that's okay?" She winced when her voice quivered a little as she spoke. "Terry asked me to call him if I need to talk. I think I'd like to try."

Anna and Meaghan squealed with delight. The men remained silent, but she thought she caught the hint of a nod from David.

"You won't regret it, hon," Meaghan told her a little too enthusiastically. "He's a great guy."

Susie held up her hands. "Hold your horses. I'm not planning on marrying the man. I'm not even sure *when* I'll find the courage to talk to him. I'm only considering the idea."

David leaned forward in his seat. "You've been through a lot chérie, and you're making great progress, but…" He reached into his jeans pocket and produced a small blue box tied with white ribbon. "We wanted to give you peace of mind. While we were in Paris, I had a friend make this for you."

"You shouldn't have bought me a present. You've all done too much already. I—"

"It's not a present … well, sort of." Meaghan

stumbled over the words. "Anna told us that you're not comfortable with the idea of a blood exchange. Believe me, I can understand that. I didn't think I'd ever get over my blood phobia."

"Fortunately for both of us"—David kissed his wife's neck—"you did."

"Okay…" Susie tried to ignore both the reference to blood and the intimate gesture as she untied the ribbon and lifted the lid. "A watch? Thank you. It's beautiful, but what does it have to do with a blood exchange?" She dropped the box in her lap. "It doesn't hold blood, does it?"

"No. Nothing like that." Meaghan laughed. "David, you explain."

"It's not *just* a watch. Do you see the red button on the top?"

Susie traced her finger around the edge of the watch until she found it. "The one shaped like a heart?"

David nodded and held out his wrist. "We each have one."

"That's nice … but I still don't see the connection."

Anna piped in. "We were all concerned for you. Although a blood exchange would be the ideal way to stay connected, David suggested the watches. If you depress the red button, we all get a distress call from you. The watch has a locator. Whoever is the closest to you when the alarm goes off will be there almost instantly. Give it a go."

Susie depressed the button and instantly, the room began to buzz with the sound of alarms. Anna held out her wrist. "See! It displays your name and location. We can get to you any time, night or … actually, only at night." She wrinkled her nose at her husband. "That could be a problem."

Susie's eyes widened. "Can any vampires go out during the day?"

"Not unless they want a really deep tan," Derrick told her with a snort. "Believe me, it's not fun."

"Then I should be okay," she decided. *Should* be being the operative word. She took another look at the watch and gasped. Diamonds? "David! Meaghan! This is really too much! You shouldn't have gone to so much expense."

"Oh, let him have his fun," Meaghan teased with a shake of her hands. "He loves buying diamonds for beautiful women."

"You, my darling," David cooed to his wife, "are the most precious jewel in my life now." He drew her into his lap and kissed her so passionately, Susie expected the couch they sat on to combust.

"Oh, get a room!" Derrick told them as their hands began to explore each other's bodies.

Susie put her half-empty glass down onto the coffee table and rose to her feet. "I think that's my cue to go," she informed them.

"Don't go," Meaghan protested as she wrestled free of her husband's grasp. "We'll behave, I promise." She slapped David's hand off her thigh.

"No, it's fine. I need to make a call, anyway," she told them with a wave of her hand. "Good night, all. I'll see you tomorrow."

Not waiting for a response, she hurried back to her room, praying that she wouldn't lose the confidence to make that call.

****

"Hello, Mr. ... sorry, Terry. This is Susie Lister."

After an ever-so-slight hesitation, she heard him answer.

"Are you all right? Has anything happened?"

"I'm fine, thank you. Everything here is fine."

"Oh, good," he answered in a breathless voice. "You had me worried for a moment. I figured that if you were calling, it must be pretty important."

She sighed. How low had she fallen? Would this man ever believe that she had once been outgoing and vivacious? "No, Terry. It's all good. I just wanted to … I wondered if … could you use my help?"

Another hesitation on the end of the line almost made her regret her decision to call. Was she so pathetic? "Look, it's okay. Sorry to have bothered you—"

"No, no. Don't hang up," he shouted. "I was just a bit shocked by you offer. I was told that—"

"That I didn't leave the house?" She could barely hide the sarcasm in her tone.

"Yeah, sorry. Your offer surprised me. Of course I'd be happy to see you again, and often."

Susie felt the cold chill travel down her spine. Maybe this was a mistake? What did he think she was offering? "I don't know about often, but I had an idea. I'd planned on dropping the group therapy sessions because…" She considered sharing her intuitive feelings about Beau but thought better of it. Terry probably already thought she was crazy. "It doesn't matter why. I've reconsidered. I thought that my being there might help your case. Maybe I will hear something about your killer?"

"That would be great but … are you sure you're up to it? I don't want to put you under any extra stress."

"My sessions are during the day and I have a driver," she told him with a sigh.

Of course it would be stressful. Just getting up in the morning was stressful, but if there was something, anything she could do to rid the streets of another monster, she would at least try. While she struggled to think of the right words to convince him, he made a suggestion.

"Look, Susie. I don't know how you'll feel about this, and feel free to say no, but, maybe I could take you. We could discuss what information we need about the case on the way there and you could let me know what you find out on the way back."

The hand holding the phone began to tremble and soon her whole body shook. Cold sweat beaded on her forehead and she steadied herself against her desk as the strength drained from her legs. Would she be able to sit beside him in a car, their bodies close enough to touch?

"Susie?"

"I'm still here," she told him, her voice barely above a whisper.

"It's okay to say no. I'm not offended. We can—"

"I'll do it." The words exploded from her mouth before she could second-guess her decision. *Baby steps.* "At least I'll try."

"Good, good," he told her. "When is your next session?"

"Tomorrow. It starts at eleven AM."

"I'll pick you up at 10:30 AM, if that's okay. I know it's only ten minutes away, but we can formulate a plan on the way. Does that suit you?"

She nodded her answer, then answered, "Uh huh."

"Great. I see you at 10:30 sharp. And, Susie?"

"Yes, Terry?"

"Thanks."

Chapter Seven

You've got this. He told himself on the drive to the mansion. *Take it steady. Don't frighten her away.* He'd begun the mantra back at his home, while he showered, dressed, and as he ate breakfast. Her call had thrown him for a loop. No way would he ever have believed this beautiful, fragile woman would offer to, not only assist him on the case, but also allow him to drive her, unescorted to the sessions. This gal was tougher than her guardians gave her credit for.

"We don't underestimate her at all," the voice in his head insisted. *"Her courage and compassion are constant surprises, considering what she's been through."*

"Damn you, Corel. Can't a man have a moment's peace from you?"

David's laugh made his blood pressure rise. *"Yeah, very funny. Now fuck off and give me some space."*

The laughter ceased and David's voice deepened. *"In all seriousness, Palmer. She's surprised us all with her offer to help you. We're not sure if she's ready."*

"I understand your concerns, and actually, I was as surprised as you were when she made the offer. I won't put her in any danger, I promise."

"See that you don't," David told him through their telepathic connection. *"We're counting on you."*

"Listen, Corel. I may not know her very well, yet, but I would throw myself under a bus to protect that woman."

"It may come to that," David warned him. *"Anna thinks that evil isn't finished with Susie. Obviously we*

haven't discussed it with her, but ... look, we're going to need you to help us during the day when—"

"Yeah, yeah. Sunlight and vampires don't mix."

"Listen, Palmer. I'm leaving a package for you. This is what I want you to do…"

****

When Susie opened the door, she held a package in her small, shaking hands. *Poor kid. She's terrified to ride with me.* A ball formed in the pit of his stomach and he suppressed a sigh. When Meaghan dashed his hopes for a relationship, her rejection hurt. This. This crushed his soul. Susie's half-smile welcomed him, but the fear in her eyes warned him to keep his distance. He wondered how he could manage that when every cell in his body ignited at the very sight of her.

"Good morning." She waited for him at the top of the stairs.

God, she's beautiful. He kept his opinion to himself.

She held out the package with both hands. "David asked me to give this to you."

When he reached for the gift, his hand brushed her skin and she dropped the box. Only his fast reflexes prevented it from smashing to the ground.

"I'm so sorry," she mumbled her apology. "I—"

"My fault," he told her. "I think I bumped your hand."

She smiled her appreciation of his excuse and his heart melted. A shiver of electricity tingled over his skin and he returned the smile, wondering how sweet her lips would taste. Opening the box, he took out the watch that David had explained was a lifeline for Susie.

"Geez," he exclaimed with a whistle as he examined the stainless steel Rolex. "These Corels have great taste in jewelry."

"I know," she agreed, holding out her own wrist. "I've never owned something so beautiful before."

Ignoring the temptation to touch her wrist, he leaned in only a fraction to admire the white gold band. Diamonds surrounded the watch face and even the numerals had diamond centers. A pink heart-shaped stone reminded him of the significance of the gifts. He was thankful his yellow gold watch had a black, nondescript call button.

"My last car wasn't worth as much as this," he told her with a shake of his head. "Must be nice to have money to burn."

"They're not like that," she told him in no uncertain terms. Her instant and angry reaction took him by surprise. "They're the most generous, selfless people I've ever met."

Terry held his hand up, palm out. "I didn't mean to offend. I guess it did sound crass." He brought his hand back and ran his fingers through his hair. "I don't know if Meaghan has talked much about our childhood."

She shook her head.

"We were raised in an orphanage, she and I. Neither of us ever expected to even see houses like this one"—he motioned to the front of the mansion—"let alone Meaghan living in one. Maybe, I'm a bit jealous."

Susie raised her shoulders in a shrug. "My parents worked hard all their lives to give me a happy, safe home. I never went hungry but … things like this"—she gestured to her watch—"beyond my wildest dreams."

Terry removed his old Swatch and placed it in his jacket pocket before attaching the clasp on his new watch. "Damn. I didn't notice the time. We should get moving."

Susie nodded and hesitantly stepped outside the foyer, closing the door behind her. He wanted to offer his hand, not just for support. He craved physical contact with her. *Don't do it*, he warned himself. *She'll take off running and you'll never see her again.* Instead, he turned his back and hurried down the steps to open the passenger door of his company vehicle. Behind him, the sound of heels hitting the sandstone told him that she'd not fled. Not yet, anyway. He held the door as she climbed into the passenger seat, biting his bottom lip when he noticed the shapely curve of her calf, despite the loose-fitting jeans. As hard as she'd tried to cover her body in a shapeless shirt and baggy slacks, she'd failed miserably to disguise the beauty beneath. *If only I could tell her.* His hand itched to trace the contours of her leg. He quickly looked away, closing the door behind him, before hurrying to his seat.

Once on their way, he reminded her of the significance of the watches.

"First sign of any trouble—"

"I'll press the panic button," she answered with a hint of sarcasm.

He turned his head in her direction. "I mean it, Susie. Even if you just feel uncomfortable and want to go home, signal me and I'll be there in a heartbeat."

She took a deep breath and let it out. "I won't lie. I'm terrified to be doing this, but I have to try." Her voice broke. A sob caught in her throat as she told him, "I can't live like this anymore."

He lifted his hand slightly from the steering wheel before lowering it again. As much as he wanted to give her leg a reassuring pat, it was too soon. Instead, he told her, "You're the bravest person I've ever met, Susie Lister. Meaghan has only told me a little about your ordeal and I can't even imagine how hard it is for you to do what you're doing for me. It means the world. Honestly. I can't thank you enough."

She lowered her head and closed her eyes. When she re-opened them, tears glistened on the tips of her long, dark lashes. "I don't understand why, because I barely know you, but somehow I know I'm safe with you."

Her head turned in his direction. She reached out and touched his hand slightly, and for only a few seconds before returning it to her lap. They sat in silence for the rest of the trip. The sensation of her touch lasted the entire journey.

****

"I'll be waiting here in the car," he promised as she entered the red brick building, but the moment she lost sight of him, her heart beat double-time. *You can do this*, she reminded herself as she ascended to the fourth floor. When the elevator doors opened, she gasped. Beau stood outside the room, and judging by the expression on his face, he'd been waiting for her.

"Susie. I was hoping you would be here today."

"Hello, Beau," she mumbled as she tried to edge around him, a difficult task considering his shoulders blocked most of the door frame. Worse still, he seemed to angle his chest so it was impossible not to brush against her breasts. A wave of nausea churned her stomach and a sob caught in her throat as she rushed to take a seat between two patients. Her right index finger hovered over the heart-shaped button on her watch, even after the doctor arrived.

"I'm sorry that I'm a little late this morning," Doctor Dubois apologized. "I had an important phone call."

"More important than us?" growled the middle-aged man beside Susie, making her immediately regret her seat choice.

"Now, Harold," Charlotte Dubois reasoned in

calming tones. "Everyone in this group is very important to me."

"What was it about? This call that stole ten minutes from my session," Harold grumbled, leaning forward in his chair. His hunched shoulders and steely eyes sent a shiver down Susie's spine but the doctor appeared to be oblivious to the aggressive behavior and tone.

"It has nothing to do with this session," she told him. "And, we'll stay ten minutes late to make up for the lost time."

"I bet it has something to do with that nutter, Allan." A young woman with mousy hair and dark glasses piped up. "You know, he killed his wife."

"We're here to discuss our feelings and not gossip about other patients," the doctor informed her, "but while we're on the subject of Mr. Whittaker." She placed her notepad in her lap and glanced around the room, pausing on every face. "If he tries to contact any of you, or if you see him. Please contact me immediately."

Susie studied the faces of the other patients, hoping for a glimpse into their emotional states. Some looked excited, as though knowing a murderer gave them some sort of superiority over the average Joe. A couple of people looked frightened. She imagined that her own expression mirrored theirs. One young man with greasy, shoulder-length hair, a sleeve of tattoos, and numerous facial piercings stared blankly ahead. His vacant expression reminded her of the last time she saw Allan Whittaker. The hairs on the back of her neck stood up and her finger came close to depressing the little pink button.

"I didn't catch two buses and drag my ass all the way here to discuss that psycho," Harold suddenly barked, causing her to jump in her seat. "Can we get on with this crap so I can get the missus of my back?"

For the entire session, Harold complained how the mental exercises the doctor had given him for his anger management issues were not working. In his words, "as useless as tits on a bull." Susie couldn't take her eyes off the man with the vacant expression. She half-expected him to jump from his seat and massacre the group who were focused on the roaring man with anger problems. The only people, besides herself, who weren't focused on Harold were Doctor Dubois and Beau. The doctor's gaze flittered between Susie and Harold, as if she were waiting for Susie to react. Beau's attention remained focused on her face with intermittent glances down the length of her body. Bile rose from her stomach, burning her throat as she fought to keep the acid reflux down. She wrapped her arms over her chest as his gaze wandered over her breasts and she wished the session would end.

When the discussion finished and the doctor called time, Harold abruptly left. A few people lingered to chat and Beau made a beeline for Susie. Every cell in her body screamed for her to run, but her legs remained rooted to the spot. She closed her eyes and reminded herself of the conversation with Anna. *He's just a handsome man who happens to be attracted to you. Not a monster.* Sadly, the words were little comfort to her erratically beating heart. She turned toward the doctor, hoping to discuss the matter of Beau, but Dr. Dubois appeared deep in conversation with another patient. Greasy hair guy. He stared intently into the doctor's eyes as she spoke, occasionally nodding. The doctor glanced around the room, reached into her jacket pocket, and handed the man what looked like a small vial. He took the vial without saying a word and left the room. *I must tell Terry.* Susie spun on her heels and slammed straight into a muscular, male chest.

"Whoa, little lady. Where are you off to in such a

hurry? I was hoping we could go for a drink. I'd enjoy getting to know you a bit better."

Beau's perfectly straight, super-white teeth mesmerized her and his deep, almost black eyes should have been comforting, but her insides turned to liquid. *Just a man, just a man.*

"No, thank you," she answered softly, "I have a friend waiting to give me a lift home."

"Perhaps another time." He snatched her hand before she had time to react, raised it to his mouth, and kissed her knuckles. "I would so like to know what goes on in that pretty head of yours."

She pulled her hand back and placed it inside her cardigan pocket. "See you next week," she called as she rushed for the elevator, depressing the "close door" button before anyone else could enter behind her. By the time she reached the car, she could barely speak.

****

"What happened?"

Susie had almost run to the passenger side of the car and jumped in before Terry had a chance to open her door. *The poor kid looks terrified.*

"Please take me home," she almost sobbed as she snapped on her seat belt.

He considered repeating the question, but Susie's body language warned him to give up. She sat staring straight ahead. An occasional whimper slipped from her lips. A single, glistening tear trickled down the curve of her cheek and leaped from her chin. She needed time.

Halfway home, she opened up to him.

"I'm sorry, Terry. You must think I'm a real wuss."

He resisted the urge to touch her leg. "I think you're very brave and you're handling a tough situation with dignity and grace."

She rewarded him with another half-smile and his stomach did a back-flip. *What I'd do to see her really smile at me.*

"Something happened in the session today, something that might relate to your case."

"Go on."

"There was another strange man there today. He acted like Allan did last session, you know, staring ahead, vacant expression."

"Did he say anything?"

She shook her head. "Nothing, nada, not a word. I don't mind telling you, he creeped me out." She shuddered in her seat.

"That's a start, anyway." Terry let out a deep breath. Not much of a lead but something to work with.

"There's more," she told him, her voice sounded higher pitched, almost excited. "After the session, I saw the doctor hand the guy a vial from her pocket. It all looked a bit suss, like it was meant to be secretive."

Terry sat upright in his seat, nodding as he processed the new information. "Great work, Susie. See, this is why we make a good team."

She raised one eyebrow, her eyes narrowed, and a nervous giggle escaped before she covered her mouth with her hand. "We're a team?"

"Aren't we?"

Susie rubbed the back of her neck. "I guess I hadn't thought of it that way before."

Idiot. You've frightened her off. "I thought … when you offered to help me, I … I thought you meant for the duration of the case."

She sat quietly for a few minutes, staring out the passenger side window. The wait seemed like eternity before she spoke again.

"If I'm ever going to learn to function normally

again…" She turned her head to face him.

A beautiful stillness had come over her features. No artist could ever do this face justice. No angel could ever look as pure and good. No wonder his heart skipped a beat.

"I must learn to be brave."

He opened his mouth to speak, but she held out her hand, palm out. "Do you think we could go somewhere? Somewhere quiet where we can talk?"

His immediate thoughts were to take her to his apartment. Soft music, a glass of red, slipping into something more comfortable…

Ass. He bit his bottom lip and forced the arousing image from his mind. *Time, Palmer. You must give her time to heal.* "Do you have anywhere in mind?"

****

"Thanks for the lunch," she mumbled with her mouth half-full of fries.

He marveled at how her persona could switch from fragile to seductive, and yet still remain adorable. Her ketchup-smeared lips were so tempting. As much as he detested tomato, the condiment called to him, *Taste me.*

"Anna and I always stopped here for a breather after our run." She motioned to the almost empty bag of fries and the half-full chocolate shake. "I'll probably need to run home to burn off these calories."

Terry patted his distended belly. "It's been a while since I ate fish and chips at the beach. I don't remember the last time I was here."

"There's something comforting about the sea."

Her expression softened as she looked out to the horizon. Her shoulders relaxed, and as she leaned back on her elbows, he watched her dig her toes into the sand. Reluctant as he was to spoil her mood, his inquisitive nature reared its ugly head.

"What did you want to talk to me about, Susie?"

She sat up, drawing her knees under her chin to hug her legs. Her eyes narrowed before she turned her face slightly away from him.

"You seem like a nice guy…" she began, and the food in his stomach curdled. *Great! Here we go again. You seem like a nice guy, but I'm not interested in a relationship with you.*

"…so I'm hoping you're also a good listener."

Damn. That's a surprise. He sat forward and hesitantly raised her chin with his index finger. "You can trust me, Susie. I'm like a steel trap when it comes to secrets."

Despite the slight tremble at his touch, she didn't pull away. Tempting as it was to leave his hand on her delicate face, he slowly dropped it to her knee, gave her a soft pat, and rested it back on his own thigh.

"It's not so much a secret," she informed him, the corner of her mouth curling slightly into a grimace. "It's more…"

He watched her shoulders rise again, her body raise an invisible barrier around itself. Her eyes glazed a little, then brimmed with tears.

"You don't owe me any explanations," he told her. "If you're not ready to talk, that's okay."

She shook her head. "No. You don't understand. I need to talk about it." Her sorrowful expression broke his heart as she told him, "Anna and the others feel responsible for what happened to me. I see the pain in their eyes whenever they look at me so I can't talk to them about it. I'd only make them feel worse."

"It? You mean your abduction?"

She answered with a nod. "I only agreed to the visits with Doctor Dubois to appease them. Our sessions are pretty useless. How can I tell her what really happened? They'd lock me up and throw away the key."

"What? You don't think she'd believe in vampires?" He tried, unsuccessfully to stifle a chuckle. She reacted with a giggle of her own.

"You do understand."

"More than you know." Vampires, demon dogs, devil worshippers. All real. All beyond belief. Walking nightmares.

"I blame myself," she suddenly blurted. "I trusted him. He was handsome and charming and I trusted him. How could I be so stupid?"

Terry shook his head and resisted the temptation to take her into his arms. So fragile. So beautiful. So broken. "Those vampires could charm the pants of anyone. It wasn't your fault that you fell for one."

"No, Terry." Her head cocked slightly to the left as her right eyebrow lifted. "It wasn't a vampire who deceived me. He was human. A human male."

"I … I guess I just assumed."

"I thought they must have told you my story." She shrugged and asked, "What do you know?"

Terry scratched the back of his head and wondered what to say. He knew she'd been held hostage by vampires and severely traumatized. Should he tell her that? Would she really want him to know?

"Not much," he told her honestly. "They, I mean, David and Meaghan told me it was your story to tell, when you were ready."

She glanced at her watch. "Then, I guess I'm ready."

****

Susie drew in a deep breath and let it out slowly. He stared at her with wide, gentle eyes. Eyes that promised to understand. She hoped she hadn't

65

misunderstood his expression. *Here goes.*

"One of the girls at the gym told me about a guy she knew from back in high school and thought we might click. I hadn't been on a date for over six months so I allowed her to set up a blind date." *Geez, how lame do I sound?* "Anyway, it started out fine. He was handsome and charming and had lovely green eyes." Although they paled in comparison to Terry, whose emerald-green eyes closed slightly as his eyebrows furrowed.

"I thought … I'm sure someone told me that it was a vampire who took you."

"No. Patrick, the blind date, turned out to be Anna's ex. He'd made a deal with the vampire to lure me away in order to blackmail Anna."

"Bastard!" Terry slammed his fists down into the sand. "How much did he get for selling you to the blood suckers?"

She shook her head. "He didn't want money, he wanted immortality."

Terry sat bolt upright, his hands dropped to his sides, and his mouth gaped open. "You're shitting me? He actually *wanted* to become a vampire?"

A wave of nausea swirled in her stomach as she remembered the conversation Patrick had with Torke, the ancient vampire. Not only had Patrick *wanted* to be turned, he practically begged for it. She barely managed a nod as she struggled to keep the bile from rising to her mouth. The acrid taste a further reminder of her time in captivity.

"You don't owe me an explanation," Terry told her as he hesitantly leaned toward her. "If this is too difficult for you—"

"No. I can do this." He had meant to touch her, to console her. She could see it in his body language. And, damn it, as much as the thought terrified her, his reluctance cut her to the quick. "I'm terrified, Terry. But not in the way they think."

He tilted his head a little to the left. "They?"

"Anna and the others." She tapped her fingers on her knees, trying to distract them from disappearing into her mouth. "I'm sure they think I blame them for what happened, but I don't … truly I don't. It's just—"

"Being around vampires brings back the memories?"

Two fingers on her left hand slipped into her mouth. It felt comforting. Helped her to be brave.

She shook her head as she lowered her chin. *Maybe if I don't look at him?*

"They're all newlyweds who can't keep their hands off each other. It's hard to watch."

"Oh." He reacted with a slight frown. Fine lines worried his brow. "That came out of left field. I'm not sure what to say." His mouth twisted a little on one side, then, he chuckled, instantly covering his mouth with his hand. "I'm sorry, Susie. I don't mean to be disrespectful, but…" The chuckle escalated into a laugh.

"It's not funny," she reminded him, but even she saw the humor in what she'd said and giggled in response to his reaction. "Okay, maybe a little." She covered her face with her hands as she felt the heat rise to her cheeks.

"If it helps, I find it nauseating myself," he confessed. "But I'm guessing that there's more to it."

When his laughter abruptly stopped, she removed her hands and turned to face him.

"Is it wrong to be jealous?" she asked. Tears burned behind her eyes, threatening to spill over her cheeks. "I feel so alone, as though I'm trapped in a prison of my own making."

She felt the pressure of his hand over her own and the instant tremor that always followed physical touch, but she refrained from pulling away.

"You're not alone, Susie. Whether you want it or not, you have many friends who are here to support you."

Tears dampened her cheeks. She swiped at them with the back of her hand. "But—"

"But you can't stand to be touched."

"Not since … you know." The drumming in her ears kept time with the erratic beating of her heart as she mentally prepared herself to confess. "There were six of them. I think Torke called them his minions. Whenever he wasn't around, they'd … they'd…"

"It's all right, Susie." He gave her hand a squeeze. "You don't have to tell me."

"If not you, who else?" she asked, her voice breaking into a sob. "I can't tell Anna and the doctor wouldn't believe me." She gazed into the emerald of his eyes, hoping, pleading to a higher power. *Please don't let him be another Patrick.*

"When they weren't biting me, draining my blood … their hands were all over me. They tore at my clothes, threatened to … do worse. Torke promised them that, once he had what he wanted, they could do what they wanted to me. Every night they reminded me of that. Reminded me of what to expect." Her voice rose in pitch until she almost screamed her confession. "I hear their voices in my dreams every night. I see the lust and hunger in their eyes and feel their icy hands on my skin. I imagine what would have happened to me if Anna hadn't come when she did." She pulled her hand away to shield her face from the pity she expected to see in his eyes.

****

Poor kid. He desperately wanted to pull her into his arms and comfort her, but even the touch of his hand had alarmed her. Yes, he'd noticed the way her hand trembled beneath his, fluttering like a little bird caught in a net. Her eyes had widened then glazed over as if she were about to faint. Her face visibly paled, making her freckles stand out like polka dots on her already fair skin. Skin that, he suspected, usually enjoyed time in the sun. Not that her skin looked sun damaged or rough. Far from it. Nevertheless, freckles gained the name sun kisses for a reason. When those vampire bastards stole her confidence, they stole the light from not only her days, but also her nights.

"I can't even imagine how horrible it was for you," he told her, "and I've seen evil in many forms." *More than I care to remember.* "But, Susie, if you let them extinguish your light, you shift the scales in their direction."

As she turned her head to face him, shards of light poked through the clouds behind her, highlighting the gold strands in her summer-blonde hair. *The fingers of God.* A gasp slipped from his lips and his body reacted with a tremor that extended to his groin. *Damn, she's fine.*

"Scales?"

What was I talking about? "Scales? Oh, yes. I mean the balance between good and evil."

"What has that to do with me?" She leaned away and narrowed her eyes as though she were trying to read his mind. For a moment, he wondered if she could. Hell, David could and did, much too often.

He rubbed the back of his neck and grimaced. "If we're being honest. I have a confession to make." He waited for a reaction that didn't come, then continued. "After our first meeting at the office, I did a bit of digging."

This time, she did react. In the few seconds it took for her to jump to her feet and stand, legs apart, hands on hips, he got a glimpse of the plucky girl described to him by her friends.

"You were investigating me?" Her blazing eyes warned him that if looks could kill, he'd be stone dead. "Why would you do that?"

He rose slowly, holding his hands palms out as he tried to explain. "It's not what you think."

"Really? What *am* I thinking?"

Terry shrugged. "Judging by the expression on your face, I'd guess you're thinking about breaking my nose."

Susie bit her bottom lip, made a choking noise, and then burst out laughing. "You really are good at gauging people, aren't you?"

Bells tinkled. At least it sounded like bells. Her laughter like music to his ears. Her smile everything he'd imagined it would be and more. If she took that swing and splattered his nose, he'd go to the hospital a happy man. A small price to pay.

"I've made a career of it," he reminded her, returning the smile. "Although, some people are harder to read than others."

She crossed her arms over her chest, narrowed her eyes, and asked, "So, you're saying that I'm one of them?"

Dark clouds began to roll in, and while they'd been talking, the sun had begun to set. Terry motioned toward the car. "It's getting late and I think there's a storm coming. Can we talk about this while I drive you home?"

The light in Susie's eyes diminished. Her shoulders ascended to her earlobes and she hugged her arms tighter around her chest. The frightened kid resurfaced.

"It's almost dark." She practically squealed as she rushed toward the car. "Yes, take me home. Please, take me home now."

When he closed the car door behind her, he felt her emotional shield snap into place and it hurt as much as a physical slap. There would be no more discussion tonight. He shook his head and jumped into the driver's seat, pausing for a moment to check on his passenger. *So close.* She sat curled into a little ball, shaking as she stared blankly out of the window. He covered her with his jacket, turned over the ignition, and began the silent journey back to the mansion.

Chapter Eight

"What were you thinking?" David growled the moment Susie disappeared into her room. "I told you to have her home before dark."

"I know, I know." Terry stared down at his own feet, his head turned slightly away from his angry boss. "We were talking and time got away from us."

David's expression softened. "She talked to you?"

"Stranger things *have* happened. I've been told that I'm not completely unfortunate looking."

"You're a hottie," Meaghan called from inside the house. "For heaven's sake, David. Invite the man in."

David narrowed his eyes and frowned as he ushered Terry inside. "If I must."

As he entered the living room, Meaghan rushed to greet him with a hug. David's eyes flashed amber, warning him to keep his distance, so he gave her a quick peck on the cheek and broke away. Tempting as it was to piss off David, common sense warned him that it wasn't a good idea to bite the hand that feeds.

"Okay, Terry. Spill." Meaghan dragged him over to one of the huge sofas and sat beside him. "I heard you tell David that you and Susie had a conversation."

"Move over," the gruff voice behind him ordered before he had a chance to speak. David brushed him aside to sit by his wife.

"David!" Meaghan yelped. "That's so rude."

"Was I being rude?" He turned to Terry, with daggers for eyes.

"He can't help it, Megs." *Dickhead.* "He feels threatened by my good looks and dazzling personality."

David's shoulders drew back, puffing out his

chest. "If anyone should feel threatened, Palmer, it should be you."

"You look a little flustered, boss?" He turned back to Meaghan, whose eyes were now as wide as saucers. "Maybe he's worried that you've changed your mind, reconsidered your decision to choose him over me."

David rose from his seat and stared down at him. "Or maybe I'm wondering why I bothered to save your life when you seem hell-bent on getting yourself killed!"

Springing to his feet, Terry bellowed, "Are you challenging me? 'Cause if that's—"

"Break it up!" Meaghan stood between them, holding them apart. Her physical strength surprised him. "What's gotten into you two? I thought we were past all this jealousy crap."

"Jealousy?"

Terry recognized the mousy little voice instantly and turned to face Susie, who stood trembling by the entrance to the room.

"It's all right, Susie," Meaghan told her in a calm voice, her palms facing outwards. "The boys are just letting off a little steam. Nothing to worry about."

Susie turned her attention to Terry. The pained expression on her face confused him. *Why is she upset?*

"You and Meaghan. You were a couple?"

"We've known each other forever. She's the closest thing to family I have."

"It's none of my business," she mumbled with a shake of her head. "I just came in to thank you for the lift today and to excuse myself." She turned to Meaghan. "If you don't mind, I'm heading off to bed."

As she headed out of the door, he called to her.

"Thank you for the talk today. If you'd like to finish the conversation tomorrow, I'll be at the office."

With a shake of her head, she called her good nights and left.

****

Second-hand Susie. That's what they should call me. She threw herself face down onto her bed and buried her face in one of the pillows. First Anna and now Meaghan. Would she always be runner up?

Patrick had told her—in no uncertain terms—that he had no interest in her at all. She was merely a pawn in a game. The bait to catch the one he truly wanted … Anna. Now, just when she had allowed herself to trust again, just when she'd begun to allow herself to imagine being with a man again, Terry had shown his true colors. He wasn't interested in her at all. Anything he did for her, any interest in her well-being was to score brownie points with Meaghan. *Damn him!* She pounded the pillow with her fists. How could she be so blind? So trusting? She'd promised herself to never again be fooled by a handsome face and gorgeous eyes. If only she'd listened to her own good advice. If only she hadn't trusted him with her story. He'd probably tell Meaghan and she'd tell the others. They'd all act differently around her from now on. She'd see a change in their behavior. They'd be uncomfortable in their own home. She couldn't do that to them, not after all they had done for her. It wouldn't be fair. No. It was time to leave.

****

Having set her alarm to wake her before the others retired, Susie dressed quickly and met Anna in the kitchen.

"You're up late, or should I say early." Anna checked her watch. "Are you okay?"

"I've decided it's time for me to get on with my life," Susie told her. "If I hadn't given up my apartment, I'd leave today but—"

"Susie. I wish you'd reconsider this. We love having you here. There's no hurry for you to move out."

"I appreciate all that you've done for me, Anna. You've all been so kind, but I've got to move on and I can't do that while I'm living here."

"Come and sit with me." Anna took her by the hand and led her into the living room. As they sat on the couch, she asked, "Why the rush?"

Susie took a deep breath and prepared to deliver the speech she'd practiced all night. It pained her to lie to her friend but, she had no choice.

"Dr. Dubois thinks it would speed up the healing process. She says that until I return to my usual routine, I won't make any headway. I have a little money saved, so I should be able to find a place pretty soon, but I'm not sure if I'm ready to return to the gym so I guess I'll need to find another job too."

"Have you ever worked as a receptionist?" David asked as he entered the room. "Sorry to eavesdrop but, you know, vampire hearing."

"I know my way around a computer and I can type at seventy words a minute."

"Great! You're hired." He helped himself to a drink and offered the bottle of Cabernet to the women.

"A bit early for me," Susie reminded him, pointing to her watch. "Hired? To do what?"

"To work at the agency." He downed his drink in one swallow. "Palmer can't man the phones and work the dayshift alone. It would really help us out."

He flashed her one of his cheeky smiles and she struggled to find the words to refuse his request. No wonder Meaghan had fallen for him. Devilishly handsome, outrageously rich, and that brazen sexuality … wow! How could any woman refuse him? The idea of working with Terry after discovering his interest in

Meaghan made her uncomfortable, but how could she reject his request for help, after all they'd done for her?

"I don't see that I have much choice." She fake-grimaced. "Fine, when do start?"

David's grin spread from ear to ear and his eyes twinkled with mischief as he said, "How about nine AM?"

"Today?" Susie yelped. "I haven't even worked out where to live yet."

"My old place is empty," Anna reminded her. "It's fully furnished and ready to move in."

"Really? I love your house." She remembered the good times with Anna's father, sharing a drink after work and many laughs, both with Jake Derwent and Anna. "But only if you charge me rent."

"Don't be silly," Anna argued. "You're doing *me* a favor."

"What? No! That's too generous. I can't—"

Anna grabbed both her hands and held tight. "It's the least I can do for you. Besides, I couldn't bear to have anyone else living there, and it breaks my heart to see it empty. You'd be doing me a favor, keeping the happy memories alive."

"There's no point in arguing with her," Derrick called from the kitchen as he made his way in to join them. "I haven't won a fight yet."

Holding back tears, Susie flew to Anna and threw her arms around her friend. "How can I thank you for all you've done for me?" She glanced in Derrick's and David's direction. "All of you."

"You can concentrate on getting better," Anna told her. "Your happiness is important to us."

"And, keep Palmer on his toes," David added. "With you there, he's less likely to slacken off."

Suddenly, working at the agency seemed like a

bad idea. A chill ran down the length of her body and her stomach cramped. How had her plan backfired so royally? She'd decided to move in order to put distance between her and Terry Palmer. How could she do that at the agency, working side by side, five days a week? Maybe it wasn't too late to change her mind?

"I can't tell you how happy you've made me." Anna squealed as she hugged her again. "I've been so worried about you. Now I can sleep knowing that you're not only on the road to recovery, you're making the house a home again. Dad would be so happy to know you're living in the house. He'd love the idea." She tightened her grip, almost cutting off Susie's oxygen. "You've made my day. Hell, you've made my year."

"Ca-an't breathe." She gasped as the realization hit home. *Damn. No backing out now.*

"Are you coming to bed, woman?"

The booming voice resounded through the house as Derrick ascended the stairs.

Anna blushed. "I guess that's my cue to leave. I'll make a few calls later and have the electricity and phone reconnected today, but there's no hurry. Move in whenever you want." She blew Susie a kiss as she rushed up the stairs to her husband, leaving Susie alone with David.

"Are you sure this is what you want?" he asked, his playful smile replaced with a look of concern. "I can hear your heart beating a mile a minute. Nothing is set in stone, Susie. You have nothing to prove to anyone."

She bit her bottom lip and considered his words. "I'm not sure if I can do this, but I have to try."

"You're the gutsiest woman I've ever met, Susie Lister, but, if you tell Meaghan I said that, I'll deny it." He grinned as he touched her arm briefly before placing his hand in his pocket to produce a set of keys. "For the time being, here is my set of keys to the office. I'll get Palmer to get another set cut for you. The password for the computer is—"

"Let me guess … kitten?"

He tilted his head to one side and raised his right eyebrow. "How did you know?"

"I've heard you call Meaghan that almost every day since I've lived here," she reminded him. "It's kinda cute."

"I think *you're* kinda cute," David told her, tapping the tip of her nose with his finger before he headed toward the door. "You'll be a great asset to our agency. Work whatever hours suit you. Get home before dark. I'll email your job description to the agency so you're up to date with what's been happening."

With that, he disappeared up the stairs, leaving Susie alone with her thoughts. *What did I get myself into?*

****

Terry hung up the office phone and plopped down on his chair. At least this time Corel had used the conventional way of communication to give him the heads up on Susie rather than use his telepathy shit. That man had a way of getting inside his head, even without the psychic connection. Last night had been a disaster. He'd let Corel rile him up. Made him act like a complete ass. Any progress he'd made with Susie had flown out the window. He could still remember the shattered look on her face before she retired for the night. She must have felt threatened by their testosterone-fueled anger. Frightened by their barbaric behavior. Why else would she have shut down like that?

Movement on the other side of the glass door drew his attention, followed by the click of a key turning in the lock. The door slowly opened and a woman stepped inside. His breath caught in his throat as his eyes followed a path from the black stiletto shoes, up the curve of her stockinged calf, to the mid-length tight pencil skirt, and higher. The beige silk blouse billowed around her ample breasts, drawing attention to her cleavage. He swallowed the lump in his throat and squirmed in his seat, suddenly constricted by the tightness in the crotch of his jeans. How the fuck was he going to be able to conceal a bulge like this in his pants?

She paused by the reception area, oblivious to his presence as she turned on the computer, and placed her handbag on the ground beside the desk. As she leaned down, her soft curls covered her face and she flicked the unruly strands of gold behind her ear before turning her attention back to the computer. He watched her in silence, reluctant to inform her of his presence, unprepared to give up his advantage. For the first time since they'd met, he could see what others had told him about her when they described a bubbly personality. She appeared confident as she typed away at the keyboard, almost happy. Suddenly, her hazel eyes widened and her hand shot to her mouth.

"Holy crap."

He faked a cough, drawing her attention. She did a double take and leaned back in her seat.

"I didn't see you there."

"Yeah, I noticed that." He rubbed the back of his neck, stalling while he formulated an excuse. "I thought I might startle you."

She shrugged and frowned. The corner of her mouth curled as she sighed. "I have that effect on people."

That's not the only effect you have on people, he wanted to say as he prayed his erection would subside before he reached her desk, carrying a strategically place file.

"Did you get bad news?" he asked, standing behind a chair.

She tilted her head and frowned. "Why do you ask?"

He motioned to the monitor. "You sounded … surprised."

Her shoulders rose in a shrug. "You mean the cussing? Sorry. I thought I was alone."

"I think I've heard worse than 'holy crap.' Give me a few days, no, scratch that … hours, and you'll be getting a real education on foul words. I'll apologize in advance." After a quick downward glance at his crotch to be sure it was safe to move, he half-sat on the corner of the desk and asked, "So, you didn't answer the question. Bad news?"

"Actually, good news … I guess."

"Sounds ominous."

"I just received my job description and a two-week advance on my salary. It's more than what I'd make in one month at the gym and I thought *that* was a great job."

"As much as it pains me to say it, Corel does pay considerably above the basic rate. I've made more in the last few weeks here than I did in six months on the force." He moved a few papers around on the desk, avoiding making eye contact as he added, "I could even afford to take someone out for a nice dinner."

"That's nice." Her focus returned to the computer screen. He'd been shut down. Never one to give up on the first try, he persisted.

"There's a great pub down the road from here. They do a great steak and fries. Maybe you'd like to—"

"I really should be reading these documents, Terry." She turned her head to face him. "I'm sure you've got your own work to do."

Despite the stern expression on her face, he couldn't take his eyes off her. *Those eyes.* So unusual a color. Were they green or brown? He wasn't sure how to describe them, and try as he might, he couldn't tear himself away, even when her brows knit and her lips tightened into a thin line of soft-pink lipstick.

"What are you staring at?"

Sprung! He lowered his chin and scratched the back of his neck. "Your eyes. The color is so unusual."

"My mother had green eyes and my dad had brown. I inherited a strange mess of both colors. Weird, right?" She looked down at her keyboard with a flutter of long, black lashes, and he gasped. How could she not know how beautiful they were? How beautiful *she* was?

"Are you kidding?" he almost shouted. "They remind me of a dish of caramel ice cream, swirled with milk chocolate sauce and just the right quantity of mint sprinkles. They're not only beautiful, they look delicious. When I look at them, I want to eat you all up."

Her mouth dropped open with a gasp and her eyes widened to almost double their size.

Immediately, he realized his mistake.

"Fuck! I'm sorry, Susie. Wrong choice of words. I didn't mean to remind you—"

A laugh erupted from her lips and reverberated down her throat, making her chest expand and contract in short, sharp bursts. Tears streamed down her cheeks as she gripped the armrests of her chair.

"Is your mind always on food?" She chuckled as she tried to control her breathing. "Or are you the big, bad wolf in disguise? Eat me up? How poetic. The ladies must swoon."

He wiped his brow with the back of his hand. *Phew! Nearly blew it again.*

"I thought—"

She reached out and touched his hand. Briefly. Tenderly. His heart did a flip-flop in response.

"I know what you thought," she told him with a warm smile. "And I appreciate your concern, but I haven't completely lost my sense of humor." Wiping away a stray tear, she added, "And that was really lovely, what you said. Funny, but lovely."

"I do my best." He chuckled, grateful for the second chance. "And, for the record, I've never had the occasion to use that line before now. You really are unique. I'd love the opportunity to get to know you better."

Before she could answer, the front door opened to reveal a courier holding a few packages.

"Ms. Lister?"

"Yes."

He held out an electrical device and stylus.

"Sign here please. And here too."

He handed her a box and an official-looking A4 size envelope. "Have a nice day," he told her, but his gaze remained focused on her cleavage. When their eyes met, he blushed and after nodding briefly to Terry, he left the office.

Terry leaned over to read the envelope. "Nigel O'Brien and Partners law offices. Looks official. Have you been a naughty girl?"

"No more than usual," she teased back. Breaking the seal on the envelope, she lifted out the contents and blew out a long breath. "You've got to be shitting me."

"I think we're going to need a swear jar." Terry laughed as he waited for Susie to comment on the letter.

"Yeah, I guess you're right," she agreed absently as she focused on the documents.

Her expression troubled him. "Is everything okay?"

"What?" She briefly closed her eyes and shook her head slightly, taking a moment before continuing. "I can't believe she did this."

"Who did what?"

"Anna. She had the deeds to her father's, I mean, her house transferred into my name. She gave me a house, for Christ's sake. Can you believe it?"

"I've gotta get me some better friends." He flopped back into the nearest chair with a groan. "I thought the watch Corel gave me was something. A house? That's something else. Shit. I think you've just won the lottery." He motioned to the box. "You'd better open that. It may be a Ferrari."

She screwed up her nose and squinted. "A little small for a car. Maybe it's a hamburger? You do still have that hungry look in your eyes."

A tremble shook his body. Was it that obvious? Yes, he was hungry all right, but not for food. As their conversation had relaxed, his dick had hardened. Damn, she had a fine body. He could almost taste the salty goodness of her breasts. Feel the soft contours of her flesh under his hands.

Snatching his files back off the desk, he held them to his crotch as he excused himself.

"Well, I'd better let you get back to your work." He turned his back and called over his shoulder, "Call me if you need me."

****

Did I offend him? Susie wondered when Terry abruptly ended their conversation and returned to his office, closing the door behind him. *Guess it's the house.* He'd mentioned that he grew up in an orphanage. *Nice one, Susie. Make him feel inferior when he was going out of his way to make you comfortable.* For a moment, she considered knocking on his door to apologize but thought better of it. *Just let it go. You'd only embarrass him further if you draw attention to it.* She sat back in her swivel chair and twirled the seat from side to side as she examined the contents of the box, but she couldn't concentrate on the task. She bit her bottom lip. Her tongue slipped between her lips, moistening them as her thoughts reflected on his expression when he told her about her eyes. *They're not only beautiful, they look delicious. When I look at them, I want to eat you all up.* Not the words of a man mooning over another man's wife.

Her body tensed. If only she'd met Terry before the vampire attack, before Patrick. Damn that slimy bastard. He'd taken everything. Her trust, her confidence, her ability to feel. But, if she'd really lost the ability to feel, why did Terry's words send a wave of molten heat through her blood stream and cause her womb to clench? Why did the hairs on her arms stand on end each time he brushed past, and why did her heart ache a little when he closed the door between them?

****

Keep it in your pants, Terry reminded himself as he flopped down on his swivel chair. It was too soon to come on so strong. She wasn't ready. *Or is she?* Her pupils *had* dilated when he gazed into her gorgeous amber eyes, or was that his imagination? He ran his fingers through his hair, cursing himself for allowing the thoughts into his head. *You sound like a serial stalker.* The door between them blocked out his view but not his desire. If only he could stop thinking about her.

"*I could help you with that, Palmer.*"

"Damn you, David." He kicked the wastepaper basket across the room. "*If I'd known you would keep intruding on my thoughts, I never would have let you give me your blood.*"

"If that's your way of thanking me for saving your life, you're most welcome."

"You tricked me! I never would have agreed if I'd known what you planned to do."

David's laugh reverberated in Terry's head. *"It's not my fault that you assumed Meaghan would be the voice of reason you'd forever hear in that thick skull of yours. Do you really believe I'd allow my woman to have access to your thoughts? Your very male thoughts. At the time, most of your fantasies involved her. They seem to have changed, of late."*

Terry dragged both hands through his hair, tugging at the roots. As much as he hated to admit it, David was right. Meaghan had already chosen David over him when she convinced him to agree to a blood exchange. Chosen to become a vampire despite her blood phobia in order to be part of David Corel's non-life. If he'd refused, he'd have died in that hospital bed, never to have met Susie. Never to have been given the chance at a real relationship.

"You're welcome."

"Okay, okay. As much as it pains me to ask, if you're going to set up residency in my brain, could you at least give me some advice on how to win the girl? And don't say patience because I'm getting blue balls here. Is there any way you could find out how she feels about me? Has she mentioned me?"

"Did I miss something? Are we in high school?"

"David, so help me, vampire or not, I'll fuck you up if you keep yanking my chain. I need help."

"Calm down, Palmer. You have Corel blood in your veins now. It may only be a small amount, but Corel charisma is legendary. All kidding aside, I'll speak to Anna. Find out if Susie has any feelings for you besides thinking you have a nice ass."

"What? She thinks I have a great ass?"

"Correction, nice ass. She let her guard down the last night you were at our home. I was able to read her thoughts for the time it took for her to ogle you. It's a shame you can't do something about your face."

"Oh, fuck off, Corel."

After a final chuckle, David broke the connection, leaving Terry alone with his thoughts.

So, she likes my butt. That's a start, anyway. If he could just convince her to like his other parts, he might have a chance. David's other comment rang in his ears. *It's a shame you can't do something about your face.* Not much he could do about that, but he could make improvements to the rest of him. He grabbed his jacket from the hook, swung the door open, and marched past Susie's desk, calling out as he reached the front door. "I'll be back in an hour or so. Call me on my cell if you need anything."

****

One hour came and went with no sign of Terry and Susie began to worry. Not so much for his safety, because, damn that man looked to be in good physical condition, but for any hope of a relationship with him. Had he gone out to meet another woman? *Of course he has.* Why would he wait around for a frigid mouse like her? He had needs. Physical needs that his clipboard had failed to conceal. She blew out a breath, remembering the impressive bulge in his jeans. Recalling the urge to cup her hand over that bulge and squeeze. The urge to do more than that. Much more. Her hand flew to her mouth. *Susie Lister, you slut.*

As time dragged on, she kept busy by familiarizing herself with the office and taking phone calls. Many phone calls from concerned families. Still no Terry. Her anxiety escalated to anger. *How could you let them win? You have feelings for this man. Don't allow the evil to steal your chance of happiness. Tell him. Tell him how you feel. Show him that he's gained your trust.*

With a sigh, she resigned herself to the hard fact. It was closing time. He wasn't coming back tonight. By morning, she'd have talked herself out of admitting her attraction to him as she'd done every night since their lunch on the beach. Since she'd realized how much she craved his touch. The empty office darkened her mood but the thought of a new client arriving after hours and keeping her late, seemed worse. She marched over to lock the door and was almost knocked over as Terry strolled through. At least he looked like Terry.

"Sorry I'm so late," he apologized as he entered the office. "I didn't realize how long it would take."

"Your hair," she gasped as she realized why she'd barely recognized him.

"Do you like it?" he asked with a hint of concern in his voice.

She reached out and ran her fingers through his hair, trying to hide her disappointment. She'd imagined threading her fingers through his soft waves. Now, she'd never have the opportunity.

"Your curls."

He shrugged and screwed up his face. "I know. They made me look like a dickhead, right?"

She shook her head. "I liked them." *And I like you*, she wished she had the confidence to add.

"That sucks," he groaned. "I should have known better than to take Corel's advice."

Susie frowned. "David told you to cut your hair?"

"He suggested a makeover." He did a slow turn, modeling a new assemble. "What do you think?"

She snorted, locking the door before returning to her desk. "I think David Corel should mind his own business. The new clothes are very lovely and suit you, but I don't know why you needed to change your appearance. You were perfect the way you were." She stopped at the desk, suddenly conscious of her words. Hesitant to face him.

He cleared his throat. "You think I'm perfect?"

Leaning on the desk for support, she took a deep breath and let the words spill out. Words she'd longed to say.

"Maybe not perfect, but I think you're beautiful. Inside and out."

"I've never been called beautiful before but…"

She felt his hands on her upper arms.

"I'll answer to anything you call me, honey. Anything at all."

He turned her to face him and lifted her chin with the finger. The gentleness in his touch almost reduced her to tears.

"I really want to kiss you now," he told her.

She nodded her approval and he closed the gap between them, tenderly, hesitantly, brushing his lips against hers. She waited for the impulse to pull away. It didn't come, even when he slipped his tongue inside her mouth, deepening the kiss.

Her hands cradled his head, holding him while his hands glided down the small of her back and further to cup her bottom. She could feel the hem of her skirt lift ever so slightly as his fingers traced her thigh. A shudder shook her body and he instantly pulled his hands away, breaking contact with her lips, stepping away.

"I'm sorry. I don't want to pressure you." He shook his head. "You have complete control, I promise. We'll take this as slow as you want." He slipped a finger inside the collar of his shirt and scratched the skin on his neck. "I won't lie to you. I want you. I want you so bad it's killing me, but it's not only the physical thing. I feel a real connection to you that I don't want to screw up by rushing you into sex. Give me some encouragement, some kind word that'll let me know you feel the same and I'll wait for you. I'll wait forever."

She reached up and touched his cheek. Those eyes. Those beautiful, kind, eyes. If eyes really were windows to the soul, Terry was indeed perfect.

"I want you too," she told him. "But … I'm afraid."

"I'd never hurt you—"

"I know you wouldn't." She brushed a soft kiss on his lips. "I'm afraid that it's too soon. Afraid that if I rush into this, I may relapse and I don't want to lose you."

"You won't lose me. Not now that I know you have feelings for me too. Still, I think you're right. We should take things slowly. Wait until you've completely recovered." His words sounded confident. His expression depicted a different emotion. A look of disappointment that hurt her heart.

She knew exactly how he felt.

"Let's get out of here," he suggested. "How about dinner?"

She answered with a nod and a smile.

"Give me a minute to turn off my computer." He kissed her forehead before heading into his office. She watched him walk away and in that moment, she knew she'd made a mistake. There would never be anyone as kind, sweet, and understanding as Terry. He *would* wait for her. The question was, could *she* wait? He'd stolen her heart, long before she'd been prepared to give it. Her body had not only accepted the touch of his skin, she craved it. There was no denying the truth. She wanted him. Not in a year, a month or even a week. She wanted him now.

Her heart skipped a beat, then made up for it with two extra beats. *No, it's not a heart attack, you won't die if you do this.* Slowly, she made her way toward his office, her hand shaking as she pushed open the door. *Will he think less of me if I throw myself at him?* She stepped inside the office, full of self-doubt, trepidation, and an arousal so strong it soaked her panties. He looked up from his desk and his eyebrows knit with concern. "Do you need something?"

Her breath hitched. *Yes, I need something.* The gap in his cotton shirt revealed a few curls of blond chest hair and her fingers itched to twirl them between her fingers.

"I've been thinking," she told him as she rubbed the back of her neck, allowing her hand to move down, over her neck, and down the front of her blouse. His eyes followed the movement of her hand as her fingers paused at the top button and when she licked her lips, he gulped.

"I'm listening," he told her with a crack in his voice.

She drew in a breath and let it out slowly as she told him, "Screw waiting."

His eyes widened. "Do you mean what I think you mean?"

She answered with a nod, biting her bottom lip as he rose from his desk, the bulge in his trousers assuring her of his own arousal.

He reached her in three strides. She wrapped her arms around his neck, cupping his head in her hand as he pressed his lips to hers. She opened her mouth as he deepened the kiss, slipping his tongue between her lips. His breath tasted of peppermint. She savored the sweet taste as she drew his tongue into her mouth, lapping the moisture as if she'd been dying of thirst and hadn't realized until now. *Oh, God, I need this.*

"You knew I'd come to you," she groaned into his mouth.

"Hoped," he told her as his lips left her mouth to nibble her earlobe. "Hoped and prayed."

"That is such a good answer." She grabbed his head, forcing him to face her, forcing his mouth back to hers, where it belonged. His tongue explored the inside of her mouth and she groaned his name as his hands tugged the hem of her skirt, drawing it up to her waist. A flood of damp heat rushed through her body, pooling between her legs, and she knew her panties were toast. Obliterated. With a swipe of his hand, he cleared the desk of all its clutter. He lifted her, stripping her of the sodden panties as he positioned her on the edge of the desk.

She whimpered as he unclasped her bra and splayed his fingers over her bare breasts, squeezing them, molding them, rolling her nipples between his fingers. Her head fell back with a moan and she closed her eyes as his lips traced the curve of her chin, down her neck to the junction just above her collarbone. Teeth lightly scraped the skin on her throat. She gasped and opened her eyes. He broke contact with her skin. A flicker of apprehension flashed in his eyes. Genuine concern. It made her want him all the more. "Please, don't stop."

As he fumbled with the buttons of his own shirt, she unzipped his fly and slid her hand inside his new trousers. *Holy cow!* She bit her bottom lip. *Big.* His cock trembled inside her clenched fist and her body reacted with another wave of damp heat. As if he'd understood her concern, he slipped a finger inside her, then a second, stretching her, teasing her, while his thumb strummed her throbbing clit. The pressure inside her built as the walls she'd erected to protect her heart came crashing down. *Close. So close.*

"Inside me. Now," she ordered, her hands

gripping his firm buttocks, nails digging into his flesh. Drawing him to her.

With a grunt, he laid her down on the desk, positioning himself between her legs. She wrapped her legs around his waist, hooking her ankles against the small of his back as she tilted her hips toward him. The tip of his cock tapped at her entrance and she knew she could deny him nothing. She dug her fingers into the soft, tight flesh of his buttocks, and with a thrust of her hips, she gave him no choice but to drive into her core. His groan encouraged her, thrilled her, and excited her. She held on for the ride as his flawlessly timed thrusts ignited nerves she'd forgotten existed, shattering her expectations into a million pieces.

She arched her back, moaning her pleasure in short bursts of approval as a kaleidoscope of colors exploded behind her eyes.

"Yes! Yes!"

As another wave shook her body, she thrust out her chest, gasping when he sucked her right nipple into his mouth. The warmth of his breath. The swirl of his tongue. The nip of his teeth. She came in an explosion that obliterated him in the process. His body tensed as he groaned his release. His guttural moan reverberated over her breast as he shuddered, then flopped forward onto his elbows, breathless and physically wrecked.

As she lay beneath him, stroking his damp flesh and trying to regulate her breathing, she noticed the scars on his body. Some quite old and faded. One large, still raw-looking scar stretching across half his mid-section. She gently touched her fingers to the wound, tracing it from end to end. At least four inches long.

He grasped her hand, brought her fingers to his lips, and kissed them.

"Not very pretty, is it?"

"How did you get it?" she asked, suddenly aware of her own exposed skin and her own distinctive marks.

"An old nemesis of Meaghan's thought I would look better with my insides on the outside." He paused for a moment and chuckled as if remembering a joke. She didn't see the humor.

"What about the others? The smaller, faded ones?" She slipped out from under him, gathering her clothes before scurrying to the bathroom, closing the door behind her.

He called his answer from the other side of the door.

"Gunshot wound on my shoulder, another knife wound to my right calf. The scar on my left knee is from surgery to my ACL. Too many tackles in my younger days."

He stepped back as she returned, dressed but still flushed with color from their recent strenuous activities. She opened her mouth to speak, closed it, and then took a deep breath.

"Aren't you going to mention *my* scars?"

Reaching forward, he took her hands in his and shook his head.

"Scars fade. Life goes on. You have a beautiful body. Don't cover it because of a few scars."

A few? "I cover them so I can forget what happened to me." She averted her eyes.

He lifted her chin with his index finger, forcing her to face him. Forcing her to gaze into his beautiful green eyes.

"Never forget. Never forgive. Turn your pain into anger and use it keep you safe, keep you focused. You're a survivor. Never forget that. Think of those scars as badges of honor. You lived through horrors that the average Joe couldn't comprehend. If you must let the marks define you, let it be as the strong, brave woman that you are."

Tears burned behind her eyes, blurring her vision, dampening her cheeks. *He thinks I'm brave?*

Bang! They turned toward the door as another knock shook the very foundations of the building. *Bang!*

"Get into the bathroom and lock the door!" he ordered as he pushed her into the room.

****

Terry reached inside the secret drawer under his desk, retrieved his revolver, and tucked it into the jeans' waistband behind his hip. *Probably just a client, but no harm in being careful.*

He unlocked the front door and froze.

A giant of a man stood in the doorway. His shoulders expanded the width of the frame, his head almost touching the top. Alabaster skin. Long, white-blonde hair tied in a ponytail. Piercing blue, cruel eyes that hinted his visit would not end on friendly terms. *Shit! Another vampire!*

Before Terry had time to collect his thoughts, the vampire barged past him and into the main office, turning his head from side to side. "Where is David?"

"What do you want with David?" Terry felt the weight of the gun in his belt but knew it wouldn't buy him much time if the vampire attacked. He positioned himself between the man and the office door as he sent out a mental SOS.

"None of your damned business," the giant told him in no uncertain terms. He made a move toward the office, sniffing the air.

Terry pulled out his revolver and pointed it at the man's chest. *Can't let him near Susie.*

"Not another step, asshole!"

The vampire glanced at the gun, then back at

Terry. The corners of his mouth curled into a grin.

"Really?"

In a flash of speed, he snatched the gun from Terry's hand and crushed it, dropping the pieces to the floor before grabbing Terry by the throat.

"I want to see David Corel, now!" he bellowed as he lifted the detective off the ground.

"Then turn around you, cantankerous bastard."

As he fell to the floor, Terry gasped for breath, sending his boss a telepathic message. *I can't believe I'm saying this, but I'm glad to see you, Corel."*

The vampires moved toward each other slowly. Terry planned his defense. Get Susie out of the building, break a piece of office furniture into a stake. He took another look at blondie, who towered above Corel. *Put your head between your legs and kiss your ass goodbye.*

"I told you to wait for me in the carpark," David reminded the other vampire as they gripped forearms in greeting. He motioned toward Terry with a tilt of his head. "Palmer here was preparing to stake you."

The vampire turned his head, dropping his chin and narrowing his eyebrows. His eyes stone-cold. "He can try."

Terry held out his hand in protest. "Thanks for the invitation, but I think I'll give it a miss." He raised himself off the ground and stood in the office doorframe, leaning against the wood.

"He thinks he's protecting someone in there."

David's eyes widened. "Is Susie in there?"

Terry nodded. "This … giant pounded on the door like he was trying to bring the building down. I told Susie to lock herself inside the bathroom."

"You'd better see if she's all right." David shooed him away with a wave of his hand but his expression showed real concern.

"I'm … okay."

Susie stood behind him. *More like cowered.* Her body so close, he could feel her heart beating wildly in her chest.

"I'm sorry, Susie," David told her before punching the giant on his shoulder. "Nice work, Christoff. It's her first day on the job and you almost scared the panties off her."

Christoff's expression remained stoic. He sniffed the air again. "I think you'll find her panties in the wastepaper bin."

Susie gasped.

David's mouth gaped open and his arms dropped by his sides. "Excuse me?"

"Your employees"—Christoff motioned to Susie and Terry—"they've been fornicating on the desk. I hope that's not *your* office."

"Oh, my God, oh, my God," Susie squealed as she ran back to the bathroom, slamming the door behind her.

"Who the fuck do you think you are?" Terry challenged, thrusting out his chest in the hope of looking at least a little intimidating. "How dare you embarrass her like that!"

David stood between them.

"I'm afraid my old friend Christoff hasn't mastered social skills, nor does he have any filters."

He continued the conversation using their telepathic link. *"Seriously, Palmer? You screwed her on the desk?"*

"It just … happened. It wasn't her fault, Corel. Don't punish her, punish me."

"Punish? Congratulate seems more appropriate. Both of you have been wound so tight, I was expecting you to self-combust. Seriously, though. It's a big step for her to trust you. Don't let her down."

Terry gazed over at Christoff who had wandered back into the hallway.

"I have a feeling that your friend there may have driven our progress back a few steps. What the fuck is he doing here, anyway?"

"We'll discuss that later. I think it's best if we leave. Christoff's presence is only likely to worry Susie further."

Terry nodded. Biggest damn man he'd ever seen. *"Sure. Later."*

****

"They're gone."

Susie tried to answer, but the words wouldn't come. She sat on the cold, tiled floor of the bathroom, leaning against the door, her hands still covering her face. If only the ground would open up and swallow her.

"Susie? Are you okay?"

"Are you sure they're gone?" How could she face David after what that monster told him? She'd never been more humiliated and yet, worse than that, the huge vampire brought back the memories she'd tried so hard to forget.

"Look. You can't stay in there forever."

The cold tiles against her bare skin reminded her of the vampire's statement. *I think you'll find her panties in the wastepaper bin.*

Can I die of embarrassment?

"I need my handbag," she told him, remembering that she always kept a spare pair of panties in case of menstrual emergencies.

What was it that Mom always said? Make sure you're always wearing a clean pair of panties in case you get hit by a bus. Or in Mom's case, a semi-trailer. Unfortunately, clean panties would not have saved Mom or Dad. They were killed instantly, leaving an eighteen-year-old only child without parents, without a home, insurance, or any type of inheritance to support her while she grieved her loss. She cupped her hands to her face, trying to block out the memories that seemed to be flooding back. *Why is this happening to me?*

The soft knock on wood shocked her back to reality.

"Here's your purse."

Slowly rising to her feet, she unlocked the door and opened it slightly, leaving only enough of a gap to allow Terry to pass her handbag. As she clutched the handle, he placed his hand over hers.

"I'd never let anyone hurt you, honey. I promise."

"Please," she whispered, "just give me a few more minutes to straighten myself up."

"Sure," he said as she closed the door, locking it once again. "Take as much time as you need."

Time? She shook her head. How much time would it take to erase all the horrors of her past? The death of her parents. Patrick's betrayal. The vile creatures who'd stolen her independence. What chance did she have while surrounded by their kind, day and night? A shiver ran through her body. If both David and the other vampire were here, it must be dark outside. Rummaging through her bag, she found the spare panties and wiggled into them, adjusting her skirt and smoothing out the wrinkles. She caught her reflection in the mirror and gasped. Pink splotches stained the pale skin on her neck. Love bites. She opened her blouse a little, noticing more marks on her breasts, a deeper color than her nipples. She thought of Terry. His mouth on her bare skin, sucking, nipping, pleasuring her beyond anything she'd ever experienced. Terry. The man who brought her back from the brink of despair. Who taught her how to trust. Who waited outside the bathroom door to escort her to dinner.

He'd protect her, he'd promised as much. But, she'd seen the strength of the monsters who walk the streets at night. Monsters who preyed on the weak and defenseless. This Christoff towered above the others, and if eyes truly were the window to the soul, he was a killer, through and through. Even the thought of him turned her blood as cold as his glacial stare. How often would she be forced to share an office with him? What would happen if she found herself alone with him? This wasn't going to work.

As she flung open the door, Terry jumped back, narrowly avoiding an injury.

"I can't stay a moment longer."

Chapter Nine

Susie opened the door and almost dropped her bag of groceries. *God bless her.* She stepped inside, ushered Terry in, and dead-bolted the door behind them before taking a better look at her new home.

"Nice digs."

As she placed the groceries onto the marble kitchen benchtop, she had to agree with Terry's observation. Although the furniture was her own, they looked almost lost in the large room. There was something comforting in seeing her own stuff after spending months living with the Corels. *My books, my couch, my cabinets.* She took the milk from the gray plastic shopping bag and turned to the fridge. Her fridge. Her *fully stocked* fridge. She shook her head. *How did I get so lucky to have a friend like Anna?*

After organizing the food and sundries, she took Terry on a tour of the house. Anna had arranged the furniture exactly as it had been in Susie's old apartment, making everything both familiar and comfortable. But, despite the homey feel of the place, her body trembled as shadows cast strange reflections across the floor. Nighttime. A shiver shook her body and she hugged her arms as the realization hit her. *My first night alone.* After the kidnapping, she had spent the first few weeks at the hospital before Anna and Derrick took her to live with them. Although they were rarely awake at the same time, she always knew that while she slept, they watched over her. *Maybe moving out so soon was a mistake?*

She checked her watch. Seven PM. Her mind raced. *Would Anna be offended if I changed my mind?* She thought of all the things Anna had done for her already when she should have been spending the time with her new husband. They *were* newlyweds. Meaghan and David would probably appreciate a little more privacy too. *David!* Her hand shot to her mouth and she cringed, shutting her eyes tight to squeeze out the memory. *No use.* She could still see the startled expression on David's face. Hear that horrible man telling him how she and Terry "fornicated" on the desk. *Fornicated! Ah!* What was she going to do? *I can't go back to work and face David. I can't go back to the mansion.* By now, they would all know what had happened. They would be understanding and thoughtful. Probably even pretend it didn't happen. But it did happen, and God help her, her body still tingled from his touch.

As if on que, he squeezed her shoulders.

"You hardly said a word during dinner."

"I'm sorry, Terry. My mind was elsewhere."

"I feel like such an asshole." He dropped his hands, scratching his head as his face wrinkled in concern. "It was too soon. I shouldn't have forced myself on you like that."

"I don't remember anyone forcing me to do anything," she responded with a shrug of her shoulders, suddenly conscious that she was still wearing the same clothes he had removed earlier. A shiver shook her body. She closed her eyes and tried to ignore the heaviness in her breasts. The moist heat between her thighs.

"I really fucked up!" he bellowed, dragging his fingers through his wavy, blond hair. "Shit, sorry, I shouldn't have said fuck … I mean—"

"It's okay." She giggled. "It isn't like I haven't used those words myself." She turned on the living room light and motioned to the couch. "Can I get you a drink?"

"I could really use a stiff one." His mouth gaped

open. "Oh, fuck! I didn't mean … oh shit. I've done it again."

Susie laughed so hard, tears streamed down her cheeks and the breath caught in her throat. When she regained her composure, she offered, "Scotch?"

"Please." He slumped onto the couch, holding his head in his hands. "As you may have guessed, I didn't have a refined upbringing like Corel. No one to teach me the polite way to speak to a lady."

Pausing before entering the dark kitchen, she flipped the light switch, glanced around the empty room, and headed for the pantry where she had earlier spotted a bottle of scotch. *Thank you, Anna.* She poured the drinks, handed him a glass, and sat beside him on the couch. "What sort of upbringing *did* you have?"

He took a big swig, half-emptying the glass before answering.

"My parents died in a fire when I was only two. I spent most of my life in an orphanage. The people there were pretty cool, but it's not like they went out of their way to make the place like a happy home. If it wasn't for Meaghan, I probably would have turned out worse than I am."

"Meaghan is an orphan?"

"Yeah." He took another sip from his glass. "She was a baby when she arrived. I've looked out for her from that day until … until Corel staked his claim."

"You've loved her all this time." *Of course he has, you idiot. She's beautiful.*

His head bobbed slightly. "But, as it turns out, she never felt the same."

"Bummer." Susie finished her drink in one gulp, rose from her seat and walked back to the kitchen, returning with the bottle of scotch. She refilled both glasses and gazed at him thoughtfully. "May I ask you a question?"

"Fire away."

"If it's painful being around her, now that she's with David. Why are you working for them? Isn't that awkward?" She handed him his glass and sat with her knees almost touching his.

"There was no use staying away. I can't get David out of my head."

Susie leaned back against the back of the couch. "Oh."

Terry's eyes widened. "No, no, no. I meant it literally. We have a mental connection."

"Telepathy? I seem to remember Anna telling me."

He sighed. "Since he saved my life. He gave me some of his blood and now we're tied by a sire bond."

"Anna offered me the same thing after, you know. I couldn't do it."

"I didn't have much choice." He took another sip of his drink. "They told me that I was at death's door. I wasn't ready to bite the bullet."

She leaned forward and placed her hand on his knee. She'd been there, done that. "I'm surprised that he didn't offer to turn you, make you immortal."

"Even if he had, I wouldn't have accepted."

"The drinking-blood thing?" Her tongue poked out as she shuddered.

"No. That doesn't bother me too much." He paused for a moment. "This is going to sound lame but … I want to have kids someday. I want a family of my own and, as far as I know, vampires can't reproduce, not in the conventional way."

I didn't see that coming. "I'd never considered that aspect of immortality." She removed her hand from his leg and dropped it in her lap. "I don't mean to offend you, Terry, but I'd never have pegged you as a family man."

He smiled. If she could call it a smile. More like a twisted smirk.

"I've never admitted that before, not even to Megs."

"Why?"

"Probably because I expected the reaction you just had." He shrugged his shoulders. "I know I come across as a badass sometimes, but the truth is, I've dreamed of being part of a family since I can remember."

"That's a pretty nice dream." She took a sip of her drink. "I'd love to have kids one day. Two, maybe three."

He nodded. "Three. Two girls and a boy. Do you have any siblings?"

"Nope. Only me." She took the empty glass from his hand and refilled it, ignoring the shiver that traveled the length of her spine. Three? What had he meant by that? Was he giving her permission or...? *You're reading too much into this.*

"My parents always joked that they had enough trouble keeping up with me. Another kid would have been exhausting."

He relaxed back into the couch, resting his arm across the headrest, looking very much like he belonged in the room. In the house. In her life. She quickly looked away.

"You and your parents sound close. I envy you."

"We were." She swallowed a gulp of her drink, and along with it, the pain rising in her throat. God, how she missed them.

He sat forward. His green eyes filled with compassion and something else. She'd seen that look earlier in the day. Right before they had crazy monkey sex on the desk. Heat flushed her cheeks, the warmth spreading over her body. When he reached forward and grasped her hands in his, her toes curled in her shoes.

"I'm assuming it was an accident?"

She nodded. The pain of the passing was as fresh today as it was seven years ago.

"They were sideswiped by a semi-trailer."

The pressure around her hands increased. "I'm sorry, Susie. I wish I could say something philosophical, but I find most of that stuff bullshit. 'Better to have loved and lost than never to have loved at all.' What crap! Having your heart torn and being told that at least that shows you have a heart is rubbish. I'm lucky. I've never felt loved so I've been spared the pain of losing someone. You're such a sweet kid. It doesn't seem fair for life to throw you all these curve balls."

"And you, Terry Palmer, are a smooth talker." She lowered her head but couldn't stop the smile curling one side of her mouth. "Which is one of the reasons I can't work with you."

"You don't like me?" He feigned a pout.

She resisted the urge to bite his bottom lip. "We both know that isn't true," she reminded him, dragging her hands away from his grip. "I would never throw myself at someone I didn't like."

"So, you *do* like me." His eyes twinkled with mischief and she knew they would be her undoing.

"That's beside the point." She crossed her arms and tried to ignore the puppy dog expression. The bulge at the crotch of his jeans proved harder to ignore. When her tongue darted out and moistened her lips, he squirmed in his seat and gulped.

"What if I promise to behave at the office, keep everything professional? Will you stay?"

She rose from her seat and paced the room, wringing her hands as she glanced out the window behind his head. *Getting darker*. Tiny hairs prickled the back of her neck. Where they being watched?

"Susie?"

She turned. "What?"

"You've gone pale. Are you all right?"

"I ... yes, I'm fine."

"Well?"

"Well, what?"

He let out an audible sigh and rose from his seat to stop directly in her path. "Will you come back to work if I promise to 'keep it in my pants?'"

"What about that horrible man, that vampire?"

Gently grasping her shoulders, he looked directly into her eyes and promised, "He won't bother you at work again. Corel gave me his word. And he also promised that no one, including Meaghan, will know what happened today."

When her right index finger disappeared into her mouth, he took her hand and kissed her fingers.

"The way you constantly chew on these gorgeous digits, they must be delicious." He drew her hand into his mouth and, in turn, tasted each finger.

"Mmm," he hummed, after tasting the last one and moving on to the inside of her wrist.

Her womb clenched as he kissed a path from her wrist, down the inside of her elbow, and up to her shoulder and neck. He cupped her head in his hands, maneuvering her face to access her lips, exploring the inside of her mouth with his tongue. Unravelling her resolve to resign.

"You said..."

"I said at work," he murmured as his fingers threaded through her hair, lightly tugging as he drew her hair back to expose her throat, "this isn't work."

She wanted to argue, really, she did, but the words

refused to leave her mouth the moment his lips reached her collarbone. His fingers moved fast, unbuttoning her blouse, unhooking her bra, tracing the flesh of her breasts. A whimper slipped from her lips as his tongue flicked the areola before playfully biting her nipple. His large hands cupped her bottom, drawing her hips up to meet his arousal. His very impressive arousal.

"Bedroom?" he asked as he lifted her, wrapping her legs around his hips.

With effort, she raised her arm and pointed down the hall before curling it around his neck. Holding him. Enveloping him. Taking pleasure from him as his mouth worshipped her breasts.

As he strode down the corridor, the fingers on his right hand crept inside her thigh, teasing her, testing her, finding her ready and more than willing. Another pair of panties obliterated.

"Hurry!" she groaned as he slipped, first one digit, then two inside her, using her own arousal to lubricate her sensitive clit and push her to the edge. "I'm—"

"Not yet," he told her as he placed her on the bed. "This time we're going to do it right."

"Right?" she asked as he unbuttoned his shirt and fumbled with the buckle of his pants. Despite the battle scars, his tanned body epitomized masculinity. She'd seen plenty of great bods in the gym, but this? This body rocked. Her hands itched to trace his skin, from his broad shoulders to his washboard abs and tight butt.

"Last time we rushed," he told her when he finished undressing. "I need to see you. Every last inch of you."

His erection bobbed inches away from her face, tempting her, but she knew she was past the point of no return. She needed him inside her. Now. She almost tore her skirt in her rush to unzip it, but, thankfully, it survived. Her panties didn't make it. He tore the thin fabric in his effort to assist her and discarded them with an excuse.

"I like you better without them," he told her as he placed his hands on the inside of her thighs, spreading her legs as his face moved agonizingly slowly toward her. He licked his lips. His hooded eyes and cheeky smile telegraphed his intentions.

"I bet every part of you tastes delicious."

She closed her eyes, shuddering as his tongue did wicked things to her body. Pleasuring her, tormenting her. Satisfying her, over and over again.

"You should teach classes in this." She gasped as she caught her breath.

"That's just foreplay." He smiled as he crept along her damp body, lapping the excess perspiration that puddled between her breasts. "I want to hear you scream my name at least another half dozen times tonight."

Without missing a beat, he thrust inside her. Filling her body, her senses. She moved with him, against him, for him. And yes, she screamed his name that night. At least half a dozen times before daylight crept through the curtains and found them sleeping peacefully in each other's arms.

Chapter Ten

The aroma of freshly brewed coffee woke Susie from the deepest sleep she'd experienced since her abduction. Yawning, she stretched, lifting her arms above her head as she sniffed the air. *Bacon?* Opening her eyes, she took in another deep breath as Terry stepped into the room, looking every bit as delicious as the food he carried. *Damn that man is hot.*

"I picked us up some breakfast from your local café," he informed her as he handed her one of the large polystyrene containers and placed the takeaway cups on the table beside the bed.

"I hope you're hungry. I wasn't sure what you'd like so I got a selection."

"I don't think I've ever seen so much food," she told him as she checked out the contents of the container. Croissant, scrambled eggs, bacon, sausage, hash brown, and fried tomatoes. *Is he trying to kill me with kindness? My arteries may not survive the morning.* "It looks wonderful, but I'm not sure I'll be able to finish this much. I usually only eat cereal."

"You were sleeping so soundly. I didn't want to disturb you to ask what you preferred," he mumbled with his mouth full of the egg and bacon-filled croissant. "I'll remember cereal next time."

"Next time?"

He continued eating, pausing only briefly between bites to hurry her along.

"You'd better hurry and eat up if you want time to have a shower before we leave for work. I hope you don't mind, but I used your shampoo earlier. We should pick up some more before we come home."

Susie raised herself onto her elbows and sat up in bed. Her bare breasts jiggled with the momentum, reminding her of the nocturnal workout.

"Next time? Home? What are you suggesting, Mr. Palmer?"

He choked on a half-chewed sausage, coughing as he replied. "Mr. Palmer? I thought we were past formalities. I seem to recall you calling out 'Terry' over the course of the night. Many times, if I remember correctly."

She averted her eyes, lowering her chin, noticing the blush of pink coloring her breasts. Judging by the heat in her cheeks, she could imagine the color they were turning. Scarlet if temperature was an indication.

"So, you think that just because we had sensational sex, you can move in. Don't you think we're moving too fast?"

"No, I don't. Wait! Do you?"

"Yes." She reconsidered her answer. "No." With a shake of her head, she sighed. "I don't know, Terry. Last night was wonderful. *You*, were wonderful. And this…" She motioned to the uneaten breakfast. "No man has ever taken my needs into consideration. But—"

"But we'll go slower. As slow as you like." He sat beside her on the bed and took her hand. "All I ask is that you give me a chance to prove I'm a good guy. You can trust me."

He gave her hand a squeeze, sending a bolt of electricity straight to her heart. *Don't you let this one get away!* her heart warned her. *You'll never find another man like him.* Pushing aside her insecurities, she agreed with a nod.

"What's somewhere between slow and smoking hot?"

"This." His fingers threaded through her hair,

cupping her head, guiding her mouth up to meet his. She could taste the bacon grease on his lips. Calories never tasted so good. As her body warmed to his touch, he broke away. After a brief kiss to the tip of her nose, he rose from the bed.

"Now eat your breakfast, take that shower, and get dressed before I forget my promise and join you in bed."

He turned his back to her and headed toward the bedroom door. She opened her mouth to call him back.

Back to her arms.

Back to her bed.

Too late. The door closed behind him, the moment lost.

****

Terry leaned back against the closed door and swallowed the lump in his throat as he tried to ignore the pressure in his jeans. *Down boy!* He tugged at the material at his crotch to ease the painful constriction. The promise he'd made had barely been spoken before he'd been tempted to break it. How would he ever keep his promise? How could he work at his desk without imagining her perfect bottom resting on the leather surface? Her long, shapely legs wrapped around his waist? The weight of her beautiful breasts resting in his open palms? The sight of her damp underwear discarded in his wastepaper basket?

He wondered what she'd say if she found out he'd taken the undies out of the trash and placed them in his pocket as a memento of their lovemaking. He scratched his head. *Sounds like the act of some psycho. Some asshole wanting a souvenir of a one-night stand with a hot babe.* But making love with Susie meant so much more than sex. So much more than bodies joining to experience pleasure. They had a spiritual connection. A joining of souls. In the short time they'd known each other, he knew she would make him a better person. She completed him. He reached into his jacket pocket, his fingers fondling the scrap of silk and lace. *You should give them back,* he chided himself, but his lips curled into a smile as he withdrew his empty hand from the pocket. *Maybe later.*

Chapter Eleven

"What the hell is going on?" Terry pondered aloud as he handed Susie another report to type up and file. "Has the entire town gone mad?"

Susie glanced up from her work and shrugged as she took the paperwork from his hand. "Ten new clients. That makes a total of thirty since I started work here two weeks ago. Maybe I should have held out for more money."

"You and me both, honey. You and me both." He leaned back against the filing cabinet and sighed. "I think Corel may need to hire more staff. I can only spread myself so thin and more crazies are popping out of the woodwork every day."

She reached out and stroked his hand. "You look tired. Maybe you should take a little nap at your desk."

He caught her hand and dragged her to her feet. "I think my fatigue has less to do with clients and more to do with our nightly workouts, as you so eloquently call them."

His mouth brushed her lips, softly, seductively. "I do believe you're wearing me out."

"Ahem."

Terry closed his eyes tight and tried to keep his expression emotionless for Susie's sake.

"Oh for fuck's sake, Corel. The office closed an hour ago. We're on our own time now."

"As much as I love to yank your chain, I see your point."

The loud cough resounding through the corridor gave Susie enough warning and time to sit back in her chair and resume her typing before David appeared at the office door.

"Thanks."

"It was for her benefit, not yours."

"I know. I repeat, thanks."

"You're welcome."

Terry sensed a gentleness to David's tone. A shared affection for Susie. *Does she even realize how many people love her?*

"Hey, boss," she chirped when David entered the office, but she kept her chin down and a blush of pink stained her cheeks. Terry had seen that rosy glow nightly for the last two weeks. A glow that covered her entire body. A glow often illuminated with the sheen of perspiration.

"More information than I wish to know."

"Get out of my head!"

Terry adjusted his pants and hoped that Corel wasn't able to access his mental pictures.

"Oh, I can and I did. Nice. Very nice."

"Did you want something!" Terry growled. The agitation in his voice caused Susie's head to snap up. Her wide-eyed expression showed her alarm.

"Terry?" She grimaced and tilted her head in the boss's direction. "David has every right to be here."

"Someone's in a mood," David told her with a wink and a flash of dimples. "I'm sure he has other things on his mind."

Terry squeezed his eyes shut, took a deep breath, and counted to ten before responding.

"It may interest you to know, Corel, that we picked up ten new clients this week."

David's expression quickly soured. His eyebrows knit and his smile tightened into a thin line.

"This is bad." He ran his fingers through his

perfectly styled hair. "Email me a copy of the files and I'll divvy up the work. You two handle the day work and pass on all relevant information. I'll get my coven working the night shifts." He addressed his next statement to Susie.

"These are extenuating circumstances. There will be times when our shifts overlap. I need to know that you'll be okay if—"

"If Christoff comes in?" Susie's face paled and the light dimmed in her eyes. Terry worried that she may be about to faint but his little trouper steadied herself on the edge of the desk and lied through her teeth.

"I'll be fine, David. Really. You do what needs to be done. Don't worry about me."

"You know she's barely keeping it together," Terry told his boss through their telepathic link.

"I'll do everything I can to keep Christoff out of the office when she's here," David answered. *"But try to get her home before dark to avoid any confrontations."*

"I know Christoff can come across as a bit of a monster," David told Susie, "but he's one of the good guys."

"I'll have to take your word for that," she answered. "I find him terrifying."

"I hate to admit it, Corel, but even I find the guy intimidating. He's like a supermodel version of Frankenstein's monster. His eyes are soul-less. Should we be stocking up on crosses and holy water?"

David's eyebrows narrowed and his eyes darkened. "Considering we share a desk … an emphatic, No."

A chuckle escaped Terry's lips and the corner of his mouth curled in a smile. "Sorry, I forgot about that."

"Did you?"

"Maybe. Maybe not."

"You're walking a very fine line."

David turned his attention back to Susie. "Look. I understand your concern. I'm asking you to put your trust in vampires and that can't be easy. Don't forget"—he motioned to the heart button on his watch—"anytime you feel threatened, I'm only a push away."

"I'd like to give you a push."

"The feeling is mutual, Palmer."

"Thank you, David." Susie rose from her seat and slid her hand into Terry's. "But I'm feeling a lot safer nowadays."

He gave her hand a squeeze. "Yeah, thanks, Corel, but I've got things covered. No one is getting near her while I'm around."

David smiled. "I guess you'd better get out of here and let me get some work done, unless you're bucking for overtime?"

Without releasing Terry's hand, Susie grabbed her purse from under the desk and dragged him toward the door. "You don't have to tell me twice."

"Before you go." David blocked the door with his arm, preventing them from leaving. "I wanted to tell you both how impressed Meaghan and I are with the job you're doing for our business. Consider this a *glowing* report."

"That means a lot," Susie told him with a warm smile. "It's the least I can do after all your family has done for me."

The emphasis on the word *glowing* struck a chord with Terry. The compliment he accepted as genuine. After all, they'd both busted their buns to make the business work, but he knew David couldn't resist one last jibe at his expense. A not-so-subtle reminder of their earlier non-verbal conversation concerning his X-rated thoughts.

For Susie's sake, he smiled and nodded at their boss, but once she'd turned away, he mouthed, *fuck you*, and left the room with David's laugh ringing in his ears.

****

"How does Chinese food sound?" Susie called through the open bathroom door as Terry showered.

"Sounds great," he called back over the running water. "Don't forget to order prawn chips."

"How could I forget prawn chips?" she mumbled under her breath. Terry could eat a whole bag on his own.

The vibration of her phone startled her and she almost dropped it before answering the unknown caller.

"Hello?"

"Is that Susie? Susie Lister?"

"Yes. Who's this?" No answer. She repeated her question. Still no answer. As she prepared to hang up, the chanting began. The strange, hypnotic melody unintelligible yet oddly compelling. Her head began to nod of its own accord and she kept the phone to her ear as she slowly made her way to the front door.

Once outside, she bent down to reach the red velvet pouch hidden behind the patio pot plant, and slipped the small bag into her pocket before returning to the lounge room.

"Yes. I have the pouch," she informed the caller. "I understand."

"Hey, woman. Where's my food?"

She looked up from the phone. Terry stood in the doorway, a towel draped around his waist, his hair dripping wet, a goofy grin on his face.

"Food?"

"Our dinner. You did order it, didn't you?"

She stared at the phone in her hand. Had she ordered the food? She couldn't remember. Lifting the phone to her ear, she listened. The familiar hum of the dial tone greeted her. Had she made a call?

"Please tell me you remembered to order the prawn chips."

Chinese food. Was I meant to order Chinese?

"No, I didn't order food." *Or did I?* She reached over to where he'd left his own phone on the coffee table and pushed it at him. "If you want dinner ordered, do it yourself."

"Whoa. Where did this new attitude come from?" he protested, taking the phone from her hand while holding the other up in surrender. "It's not like you."

She tried to remember. Was he right? How should she feel?

He scratched his head, screwing up his face as he asked, "What's gotten into you? Ten minutes ago you asked if I wanted Chinese. Now you're berating me for saying yes."

Chewing on the inside of her bottom lip, she considered his statement. Had she asked or was he trying to confuse her? Fogginess clouded her memories. Was this a lie? How many lies had he already told her?

"Susie! Snap out of it!" He held her by her forearms, shaking her.

"Get your hands off me!" she screamed, pulling away from his grasp. "Don't touch me!"

"Fine," he said, holding up both hands and backing away. "I'll get dressed and we can talk about this."

He hesitated. Did he expect her to protest? What were they meant to discuss?

His shoulders slumped and he opened his mouth to speak but left the room without uttering a word. Within minutes, he returned, dressed and fuming.

"This doesn't make sense," he argued. "What have I done?"

Why don't I remember? It must have been something important, or why would I feel so upset? "It doesn't matter," she reasoned, "I need to be alone."

He looked down at his feet for a moment, then his head snapped up. "Was it that stupid comment about dinner? You know I was only kidding, right? I thought you'd laugh."

Stupid comment? Why did he look so upset?

"It was a joke. I care about you, Susie. I think I'm falling in love with you and I believed, no, hoped, that you felt the same way about me." He reached for her but she took a step back.

Beautiful words.

Beautiful lies.

Another trap.

"I'm going for a walk." She turned towards the door, anxious to put distance between them.

He rushed to her side. "I'll come with you. We can—"

"No." Something stirred inside her, pushing her to escape before it was too late. Before—

"No? Can't we even discuss this?"

She knew he needed an explanation, but she had none to give except the words, "I'm sorry."

Chapter Twelve

"What do you mean by that?" Terry roared, almost spilling his scotch.

"It was a simple question, Palmer. What did you do to upset Susie?"

"Fucked if I know." He growled, downing his drink in one gulp. He passed David his glass for a refill. "One minute she's asking if I'd like Chinese food for dinner, the next, she's shutting down emotionally."

"It sounds like she's had a relapse," Anna suggested with a shrug of her shoulders. "We shouldn't have pushed her into working. Maybe it was too soon."

"Maybe we weren't the ones doing the pushing."

Derrick cast Terry an accusing look that left little doubt as to what he was insinuating.

Terry rose from his seat on the sofa and squared up. "What are you insinuating?" *As if I don't know.*

"I saw the way you gawked at her when we introduced you. You just couldn't keep it in your pants, could you? You knew the fragile state she was in but you seduced her anyway."

A low growl resonated from Terry's throat as he approached his accuser. "Maybe we should finish this conversation outside?"

David stepped between them. "As much as I'd like to see Palmer bust your nose, little brother, we can't afford to be fighting among ourselves. Besides, you owe him an apology."

Derrick glowered at his brother. "And why should I do that?"

"Because Terry didn't instigate the relationship. Susie made the first move."

Two sets of eyes widened. Both men opened their mouths to speak but neither said a word. Terry's fist connected with David's chin.

"Ouch." David objected as he rubbed his face. "What was that for?"

"I don't know which pisses me off the most," Terry complained, tugging at his hair in frustration. "The fact that you just dissed my woman or the revelation that you were reading my mind when we, I won't go into what we were doing. Asshole! Can't you give a guy some privacy?"

"We can discuss the privacy issues later," David told him. "We have bigger problems. Your 'woman' no longer wishes to work with you."

If David had punched him in the gut, it would have hurt less. She didn't want to work with him. He flopped back down on the sofa, cupping his forehead in his hands as he leaned forward. After a few silent minutes, he raised his chin.

"I'll have my resignation typed up and on your desk within the hour."

"Like hell you will!"

"What choice do I have, Megs?" he asked his life-long friend. "I can't ask her to do night shifts and neither of you"—he motioned to her and David—"can work day shifts."

Meaghan turned to her husband for support. "Any ideas?"

David pinched his chin between his thumb and finger. "What about this? Palmer has enough work to keep him on the streets for a while doing surveillance." He addressed his next question to Terry. "Could you work from your car?"

He shrugged. "I'd have to buy an iPad or laptop, but, yes. I could easily work from home or the car.

Actually, it would save time."

"Consider it done."

David grinned but Terry found no comfort in the new working arrangements. Yes, he could work without Susie if he was forced to, but could he live without her?

"There's one more thing. Something that might not go down very well."

"This day just keeps getting better." Terry let out an audible sigh. "Fine, spill."

"You'd better have another drink first." David filled his glass before continuing. "You've got a new partner. Someone who can take over from you at night and provide extra protection."

"Oh, fuck no!" Terry slammed his glass down onto the coffee table, spilling some of the contents. "Not him. Anyone but him."

"We had no choice. No one wants to work with either of you."

"David!" Meaghan protested. "How can you say that?"

"Because it's true." He turned to Terry. "Sorry, chum but the vampires don't want to work with a human and they're all afraid of Christoff."

"Why can't I work with Megs?"

"Because Meaghan is *my* partner." David narrowed his eyes. "In business *and* in life. It would be wise to remember that."

"As if you'd let me forget it." Terry snarled under his breath. As he rose from his seat he added, "Look, I've had about as much good news as I can stand for one night. I'm going home."

With a wave of his arm, he left the room with David hot on his heels.

"I've given Christoff your mobile number and I'll have a laptop sent to your home first thing in the morning."

"Fine. Whatever."

He reached for the door handle but David grasped his forearm and spun him around.

"I'm on your side, Palmer. As much as I hate to admit it, you're a good guy. Susie will come around, you'll see."

Terry shrugged. Without reason, she'd turned on him.

"Maybe she's reconsidered? Maybe I saw a future where there'd been none?

"You're wrong," David corrected him. "She was happy. She felt safe with you."

"Then, what should I do?"

"Give her some time."

"And what about my new partner?"

David chuckled. "Space. I recommend keeping your distance as much as possible. Keep him informed of the cases and check in from time to time. Try not to engage him in conversation and you'll do fine."

"Anything else?"

"Yeah. Try not to piss him off."

Chapter Thirteen

The elevator doors opened, but Susie froze. Had she made the right decision? Patients gathered in groups outside the door to session room. Lots of patients. At least three times as many as the last time she was here. *Can't do this.*

A hand reached out and stopped the lift doors as they began to close. A hand with perfectly manicured nails and milk chocolate-colored skin

"Susie. I'm so glad you came back." Dr. Dubois warmly greeted her, leaving Susie no choice but to exit the safe confines of the elevator.

"My boss gave me the morning off," Susie told the doctor, who took her by the arm and almost dragged her down the corridor and into the meeting room. "I'm not sure how often I'll get here."

"You're here now." The doctor gave her hand a pat before leaving her alone in the middle of the room while the other patients located seats.

She looked for a vacant seat, preferably one close to the door. Close to the exit. All the seats were taken. She froze in the center of the group. All eyes on her. Everyone waiting for her to do something. Anything. But she couldn't think. Couldn't move.

"Over here!" a voice called from behind.

She turned in time to see Beau placing a chair near his own. He motioned for her to join him. She took a deep breath and forced her legs to move toward him.

"Thank you," she told him in a whisper as she sat beside him.

His broad, toothy smile should have made her feel welcome, but instead, it prickled the hairs behind her neck. She felt vulnerable and afraid. If only Terry were here to offer her support and comfort. Why had she sent Terry away? *You must stay away from him*, something inside warned her again. If only the voice would explain why.

"Good morning."

Susie's head snapped up to notice a sea of unfamiliar faces. Where was she?

She recognized the doctor's calm, clear voice. Group session? *How did I get here?*

"Are you all right?" the man beside her asked. "Your face is as pale as a sheet."

It took a few seconds for the comment to register. "I'm…" How could she tell Beau she had no idea how she got here? Did she drive? Walk? Instead, she lied. "I'm fine. Really."

"We have a large group here today so we'd best begin."

Beau smiled and turned his attention back to the doctor.

"So. Who would like to get the ball rolling?"

****

"That was interesting," Beau whispered into Susie's ear on their way down in the elevator.

She nodded her agreement. Strange group, to say the least. Most of the patients declined to speak but, those who did dominated the session with their fiery outbursts or hysterical accusations. Even more disturbing, she'd spent the entire time trying to block out an irritating humming in her head. Humming? Chanting? Maybe a whispering? Whatever it was, it made it impossible to concentrate on the rest of the group. Had they said anything relevant to the case? She squeezed her eyes tight and grimaced. Great detective she'd make. The whole morning wasted.

"You look like you need a drink," Beau told her. "There's a cozy little bar down the street if you'd care to join me."

She held out her hand, opening her palm to reveal a small brown bottle before placing it back in her pocket. "Dr. Dubois has decided to trial me on a new medication. I'm not sure alcohol and prescription medicine are a good mix."

"Coffee then?"

She opened her mouth with the intention of refusing his offer, but as she watched his head nodding, she found herself mirroring his actions.

"I guess coffee would be okay."

He offered his arm and she tentatively slipped hers into the triangular space he'd made with his elbow. As they strolled down toward the café, he stroked her forearm. She fought the urge to pull her arm away. *He's not going to hurt you.* Besides. What could he do to her in a café full of people? But with every stroke of his hand, her stomach tied another knot.

"You're shaking. Are you cold?" he asked.

"A little," she lied. Why did her body constantly betray her? Couldn't she catch a break?

In one fluid action, he removed his sports coat and draped it over her shoulders. The jacket dwarfed her, weighing heavy on her shoulders. The musk from his body permeated the woolen fabric. She found his spicy aftershave pleasant, but … wrong. Her senses rebelled. Her stomach churned. Something wasn't right. She tried to focus, find the answer in the recesses of her mind. What was it she wanted? The answer stopped her in her tracks. Terry's scent. She closed her eyes, picturing tangled sheets. The sensation of skin-on-skin contact. The sensual allure of his Armani Code as his skin heated with the rigors of their strenuous lovemaking. The heady notes of Tonka beans and spice permeating from his body. She drew in a deep breath and stopped. *Terry?*

****

Terry climbed back into the driver's seat of his company car, slamming the door behind him.

"Son of a bitch!"

He grabbed the steering wheel, his hands balling into fists around the rim, imagining it to be someone's throat as he molded his fingerprints into the leather.

Heat rushed to his cheeks. His heart thumped against his chest wall. *What is she doing with that guy?*

Anger coiled in his belly like a snake waiting to strike. *Why do all the women I love leave me for other men?* First Meaghan and now Susie. What did those men have that he didn't? He depressed the start button on the dashboard and pulled away from the curb, narrowly missing traffic. Someone blasted their horn. He opened the window and gave the driver a one finger salute before peeling off down the road.

A familiar tune interrupted the song playing on his radio. He answered the phone call using the button on his steering wheel.

"Palmer!"

"What did you uncover?" the stoic voice asked him.

Momentarily confused by the question, he asked. "Who is this?"

"This is Berg. I was told you were expecting my call."

Terry racked his brain. Berg? *I don't know anyone by ... wait a minute.* "Shouldn't you be sleeping with the worms? It's mid-morning."

"I don't sleep with worms," the monotone voice told him. "As a matter of fact, I don't sleep at all."

"Good for you, I—"

"I asked you a question. What did you uncover?"

Through clenched teeth, Terry growled, "Absolutely fuck all."

For a moment, the vampire remained silent. When he finally responded, the tone of his voice had changed from indifferent to stone cold.

"Let me assure you. I am just as vexed to work with you as you are to partner with me but the die is cast. I will speak to you later. For your sake, you'd better have some information for me."

The line went dead before Terry could formulate a decent comeback.

"Bastard!" he cursed at the stereo screen. "Who the fuck does he think he is?" He mimicked Christoff's voice, slowly repeating the words with deep, monotone emphasis.

"The. Die. Is. Cast."

Probably thought he'd impress me with his translation of Latin. Guess what? Not impressed. Yeah, buddy, you're not the only one who's heard of Julius Caesar. If only he'd had the chance to throw that little pearl of wisdom back in the asshole's face. "And who the fuck says vexed?"

****

"So, Susie. Tell me a little about yourself."

She took a sip of her coffee, giving herself time to work out a credible answer. Beau seemed like a nice man. Therein lay the problem. She'd trusted nice men before. An old adage popped into her head. *Fool me once, shame on you. Fool me twice, shame on me.* What would fool me three times be?

"Nothing much to tell," she told him, planning not to reveal much of her life. Not yet, anyway. "I'm a qualified fitness instructor but, at the moment, I'm working at a detective agency."

"Wow!" he exclaimed, almost spitting his coffee. "That's a big career change. How did you end up there?"

The familiar queasiness stirred the contents of her stomach. She'd told no one. No one besides Terry. She'd trusted him, maybe loved him, and look how that turned out. If only she could remember what he'd done to upset her. It must have been really bad for her to feel such hostility toward him. Why couldn't she recall what had happened?

"Susie?"

"Oh, sorry. It's a long story. Maybe some other time."

"When you're ready." He nodded.

She took a sip of her coffee before asking, "What's your story? I remember you saying that you left your village to move here. Did you start another business?"

He grinned. His full lips drew back to display a perfect set of pure white teeth, but rather than feel comforted by the smile, she felt the urge to run.

Teeth tear skin.

Shred sinew.

Draw blood.

She squeezed her eyes tight. *Not a vampire. You're safe.* Yet, something in his voice motivated her to keep her right hand over her left. Her index finger hovering over the tiny jewel heart on her watch.

"I have unfinished business," he informed her, "but I have taken steps to start something new here."

"That sounds exciting." And very cryptic. "I'm intrigued. Care to enlighten me?"

"Ah, but then I might spoil the surprise." He chuckled. "Who knows, maybe I can entice you to join me once I've established a following."

"Who knows," she agreed. Maybe that was a

better option than continuing to work with Terry. She checked the time. In a few hours, she'd be expected to go in to the office. Her stomach lurched. She hated the idea of working late, driving home in the evening, returning to a dark, empty house. *It was your idea*, she reminded herself.

"Do you have somewhere to go?" he asked when she continued to stare at her watch.

With a nod of her head, she told him. "I'm working the afternoon shift. I start at two PM."

"Then allow me to buy you lunch." He waved off her attempt to argue. "We can't send you off to work on an empty stomach, can we?"

****

Despite the steady stream of clients leaving their contact information and detailing their problems, the office felt empty. She missed the playful banter. The naughty innuendoes. Terry's cheerful chuckle. The clock on the computer flashed six PM, but the landscape outside the window made it seem much later. Storm clouds loomed on the horizon. As she gazed into the darkness, a sudden chill prickled the hairs on the back of her neck. She spun around and gasped.

"I'm here to see Palmer," he told her in a commanding voice.

"He's not here," she answered, in a small, terrified voice that told him much more than she had intended. Why hadn't someone warned her?

"I'll wait." He plonked himself down on the seat closest to her desk, crossed his arms across his chest and unceremoniously planted his large, boot-clad feet on top a pile of reports.

"I'm not expecting him for another hour," she said, hoping he'd take the hint and go away.

"I'll wait," he repeated, casting her a look that

curdled her lunch. His penetrating eyes drove like a sliver of pale-blue ice through her soul, and her body responded with a shudder.

She wished she could slow the beating of her heart, knowing that he would detect the erratic rhythm and be enticed to feed. Despite David's assurances, she perceived a darkness about Christoff that she couldn't ignore. His stoicism bothered her more than anything she'd experienced with her abductors. At least with them, she knew what to expect. Their menacing stances and slimy threats warned her of what was to come. But not him. He watched her. Silently. Carefully. Like a lion stalking its prey. She swallowed the lump in her throat, knowing that, should he decide to attack, there would be no escape.

He leaned in closer. His eyes focused on her face and she realized her breathing pattern had changed. Would he take her shallow breaths as a signal to attack? She swallowed the lump in her throat, wishing, no, praying for one last chance. A chance to see Terry again. A chance to forgive him for whatever it was he'd done to upset her. To tell him what she'd known since the day he brought her breakfast in bed. *I love you.* Instead, she depressed the button on her watch, again and again and prayed someone was close.

****

He burst into the office, unsure of the danger but determined to protect his woman.

"Are you all right?" he asked when he saw the ashen color of her cheeks.

She shook her head and motioned toward the unwelcome guest.

"I told you to meet me in the carpark," Terry reminded Christoff in a voice that sounded more trill than he'd planned.

"Perhaps you've mistaken me for your lapdog," the vampire suggested as he rose to his feet, towering above the detective. "I don't take orders."

As much as he wanted to put the guy on his ass, Susie's body language warned him to keep his mouth shut. Besides, he might be angry, but he wasn't stupid. He couldn't win that fight.

Something shot past him, followed closely by another. Had the storm outside become a tornado?

"What's going on here?"

Terry spun around, fists raised, to face not only David, but the entire Corel family.

Anna had an arm around Susie. A pang of jealousy sliced through him. *That's my job.* He turned and pointed an accusing finger at Christoff who seemed nonplussed about the congregation of agitated people. "He scared the bejesus out of Susie."

"I assure you, I did no such thing," he said as he rose to his feet and straightened the wrinkles from his tailored trousers. "I barely said a word to his woman." Turning his attention back to Susie, he asked, "Did I say anything to suggest I might harm you?"

She shook her head but answered in a soft voice. "He stared at me. I thought he might…" She clung to Anna, burying her face in her friend's shoulder. Terry's blood boiled.

"Why the hell were you staring at her? That's creepy behavior, even for a human. How did you think she'd feel watching a vampire size her up?"

"She should have felt flattered," Christoff announced with a shrug of his broad shoulders. "She has the most unusual eyes. Surely you've noticed this?" He glanced around the room for confirmation before continuing. "They became larger the longer I observed them. I found them and her reaction … interesting."

"Fuck you, Lurch!" Terry stepped toward the giant and hit a solid wall of muscle when David intervened.

"You *really* don't want to offend him, Palmer."

"Offend him?" Terry sniggered. "Fuck him and the horse he rode in on."

"Lurch?" Christoff shrugged his shoulders. "Who is this Lurch? And surely the human knows I drove here in my Porsche."

"Not a word," David warned Terry when he opened his mouth to speak.

Just as well. His anger stole any intellectual response from his repertoire. His only plan had been to use expletives and lots of aggressive body language.

David grabbed Meaghan by the arm and led her toward the front door. Anna and Derrick followed behind as David called back to Christoff, "Come on, *Lurch*, let's give these two a few minutes of privacy."

"Only a few minutes?" The vampire smirked, looked from Terry to Susie, and then shook his head as he strode toward the door, turning briefly to add, "No wonder she left you."

Terry closed his eyes and counted to ten but his hands balled into fists which he slapped on his thighs.

"You promised me he'd never be here again!" Susie screamed at him in a voice that reflected both fear and rage.

He shrugged. *At least the color's back in her cheeks.* "I wasn't expecting him so early."

"Why is he here at all?" she continued while grabbing her coat from the hat rack.

As she walked past him to collect her purse, he caught a whiff of aftershave on her dress, reminding him that, if anyone had the right to be annoyed, it was him.

"Don't blame me. I thought our arrangement was

working just fine. I thought *we* were working fine. I wasn't the one who threw it all away." He kept his gaze locked on hers and tried to find guilt in her hazel eyes. Instead he saw confusion.

****

"*I* threw it away?" she scoffed. "I wasn't the one who…" *Who what? What did he do? Why can't I remember?*

"Who *what*?" He seemed equally confused. "What *did* I do? If you've found someone else, you could at least have had the decency to tell me."

"What are you talking about?"

"I know what I saw."

His face contorted into a sneer. It didn't become him. The emerald in his eyes intensified. *Jealousy?*

"I don't know what you're talking about." *Unless.* "You were following me?" Of course. Somehow she'd known. The whisper of his aftershave.

He'd been there.

Watching.

Following.

Why?

"No. I wasn't following you, not at first anyway," he objected before he turned away. "I'm still working the case." He turned back, moving closer. "You were the one who suggested that someone at the therapy sessions may have been involved. I was following up on your lead."

"Then why were you stalking Beau and me?"

Terry's eyebrows furrowed and a short, forced chuckle escaped his lips.

"So that's his name. Beau. You seemed pretty cozy together."

"Don't be ridiculous." She huffed before turning to leave.

"Ridiculous?" He leaned in and gently lifted a few

strands of her hair. "I can smell him on you."

She pulled away. "Don't you touch me."

"If you're finished with all the touching…"

When Terry turned in the direction of the voice, Susie used the opportunity to make her escape, slamming the door behind her.

****

"Why couldn't you have waited in the carpark?" Terry bellowed.

"I told you. I'm not—"

"Yeah, yeah, you're not my lapdog." *And now you've gone and made things worse.*

He ran his fingers through his hair as he paced the room, trying to concentrate on the case. "Do you have any information?"

Christoff shook his head. "All humans seem strange to me. I find it hard to differentiate between the normal and those in a trance. You *all* walk around preoccupied with your own mediocre lives, unable to see the dangers. Unwilling to interact on a personal level."

Terry stopped. *You've got to be kidding me.*

"Look who's talking. Mr. Personality. Twice now your insensitivity has driven Susie from the office."

Christoff took a step closer and glared down at his human partner. "My insensitivity? I wasn't the one accusing her of cheating."

"Who's cheating?" Meaghan stepped through the door, closely followed by her husband. "If you've hurt her, Terry Palmer, I'll knock you into next week."

Terry held his hands up in surrender. "Don't look at me. I'm loyal, boring Terry, remember? I'd be lucky to have *one* woman want me, let alone two."

David shook his head and rolled his eyes. "Cry me a river." He maneuvered himself between the two men and addressed his words to Terry. "What's going on here?"

"I don't have time for this." Christoff marched past Meaghan and straight out of the office.

"Yeah, that's right!" Terry called after him. "If you can't stand the heat, get outta the kitchen, Lurch."

"I wouldn't push his buttons," David mumbled under his breath. "He has a very low boiling point."

Terry opened his mouth for one final insult, then changed his mind. So far, Christoff had been stoic or at worst, irritating and even *that* was intimidating. He'd hate to see the vampire actually upset.

Meaghan interrupted his train of thought.

"Okay, buster. Spill. What's going on?" She pointed to the office and followed him inside. "Sit!" she ordered, motioning to his chair.

"You'd have to ask Susie," he told her, avoiding the questioning eyes staring down at him from her position perched on the edge of the desk.

"Where is she, anyway?"

"She took off when gargantuan came back." He glared at David. "I thought you told him not to come into the office?"

"No one tells Christoff what to do." David shrugged.

"So I've been told." A shiver of goosebumps trickled down his spine. Would he kill a human? *No. He's one of the good guys ... or is he?*

"That's still up for debate."

"Stay outa my head." Terry slammed his palms down on the desk and spun his chair around to face out of the window. "You may be my boss, but my relationships, or lack of, are none of your business."

The office door clicked shut. He felt the slight pressure of hands on his shoulders. Small but strong fingers kneading the knotted muscles.

"How about talking to an old friend?" Meaghan asked. "I'm concerned about the sudden turn of events. Is Susie relapsing?"

He turned his chair around to face her, shaking his head as he confessed.

"I have no idea what happened, Megs. We were going gang-busters then, pow. Punch in the guts. One minute we're discussing ordering takeaway, the next, she's distant and strange. I swear on a stack of Bibles, I didn't say or do a thing."

She drummed her fingers on his back. "Mmm. I don't like the sounds of this."

"You and me both." He leaned back in his chair, averting his eyes. "I'm ashamed to admit this, but … I followed her today. She met with one of the guys from her group therapy sessions."

"Don't get ahead of yourself," she protested with a wag of her finger, "she told us she was going to therapy this morning. Maybe their meeting was a coincidence?"

"They looked pretty chummy to me," he growled, before kicking the wastepaper basket across the room. "What am I doing wrong, Megs? Why can't *I* ever be the guy who gets the girl?"

"Maybe, you could learn to control your temper?" she suggested while collecting the spilled contents of the bin. She placed the container back under the desk and gave his leg a pat.

"Seriously, though, I don't believe you've done anything wrong. Maybe your relationship moved too fast. Maybe she needs more time."

"Time?" He sniggered. "And while I'm giving her time, the other guy will be moving in on my woman."

"So, what are you going to do about it?" she asked as he rose from his chair and grabbed his jacket from the coat rack.

"I'll tell you what I'm going to do." He marched to the door, flinging it open before calling back, "I'm going to take back what's mine."

Chapter Fourteen

"How dare he insinuate that I'm having an affair," Susie growled under her breath as she threw her handbag onto her sofa and headed for the bathroom. As she waited for the cold water to fill the vanity basin, she stared at her reflection. Wide eyes stared back at her. Her heart still raced from her encounter with Christoff, but the heat radiating from her cheeks was entirely Terry's fault. While splashing her face with the cool water, she remembered the vial in her purse.

Damn. Forgot to take my prescription.

Snatching a towel from the rail, she patted her cheeks as she headed back to her bag where she retrieved the small vial of tablets given to her by Dr. Dubois. She read the label. *Take one immediately and then one every four hours.*

Had she taken one earlier? She scratched her head and tried to remember if she'd taken one at lunch. Beau had talked incessantly during their meal, asking for details of her life, her job, her friends. She'd tried to withhold as much information as she could from the inquisitive man with the silver tongue and persuasive attitude. Had she told him too much?

Bang. Bang. Bang.

As she turned toward the sound, the vial fell from her hand and rolled under the couch. She froze to the spot, unable to move. Unwilling to see who might be waiting behind the front door.

"I know you're in there, Susie."

"I don't want to talk to you, Terry," she told him as she let out the breath she'd been unknowingly holding.

"Well, we're going to talk, whether you like it or not."

She heard the jingle of keys and a click as the door knob turned and Terry entered, closing the door behind him.

"How did you…" *Damn. He still has keys.* "How dare you let yourself in." She held out her hand, palm up. "I want those keys back, now!"

He slipped the keys into his jacket pocket and shook his head. "I'll give them back. *After* we talk."

"There's nothing to talk about," she argued as she tried to ignore the scent of his cologne, the musk of his sweat. His skin flushed a deep shade of rose. *Why is he so angry with me? I should be the one who's upset.*

He ignored her comment, stepping past her to sit on the couch. She chose the single recliner and noticed the disappointment in his expression. The drop of his shoulders.

"So … talk."

He lowered his chin and spoke in whispered tones. "Where did we go wrong, Susie? What did I do?" He raised his head and leaned forward. As he took her hands in his, he pleaded. "Whatever it is, whatever I've done. Give me another chance. Give *us* another chance."

Confusion clouded her thoughts. What *had* he done to upset her so much? How could she explain her feelings when she had no explanation? Danger hung around him like a low, dark cloud. She shook her head. "I don't know what to say."

With a gentle tug, he pulled her out of her seat and onto the sofa beside him. "Say you'll give us another chance. We bring out the best in each other. In your heart, you know I'm right."

Of course he was right. He'd awakened the old Susie. Driven the dark memories from her mind. Why, then, did she feel the urge to wrap her fingers around his throat and squeeze the life from his body?

****

Her lips parted and he expected her to speak, but instead, her eyes flared amber and she pounced, pushing him down onto his back, straddling him. She raised her blouse over her head, exposing the sheer lace of her bra, and he groaned his appreciation when she began to rock her body over his growing erection. He felt the tug of his fly unzipping and the heat of her hand on his painfully erect cock, her fingers tightening around his shaft as she pumped him for all he was worth.

"Stop," he gasped. "I'm … too close."

If she heard his pleas, she ignored them. The fire in her eyes intensified and her expression changed from aroused to almost manic. She tore at her own clothes, hurling her bra across the room, ripping the lace panties as though they were made of paper before using the damp heat of her own arousal to inflame him further.

"Susie. You're killing me." He groaned as she moved her slick clit over his engorged cock, coaxing it, teasing it mercilessly until she suddenly drove her hips down, taking the length of his arousal in one exquisite thrust. His fingers dug into her buttocks, holding on for dear life as she rode him. Her body slamming against his in fast, hard slaps. His hands moved to her breasts, hers to his throat. *Okay, that's new. Kinky, a little uncomfortable, but definitely hot.* He felt her fingers tighten around his neck, her nails dig into the flesh. His body tensed, then trembled as his cock gave a final shudder.

Her eyes widened, the pupils enormous as she released her grip on his throat.

****

Susie's heart pounded against her chest wall. What was she thinking? Thank God his orgasm shocked her out of the homicidal stupor. She'd meant to hurt him, kill him. It didn't make any sense.

Buzz.

Her phone bounced across the coffee table seconds before the ringtone blasted, followed by the caller ID.

Beau.

"Must you answer that?"

She looked down at the phone, then back to Terry. His hands were still cupped around her breasts, squeezing them, teasing the nipples in hard peaks. "Please, baby. Let's not spoil the moment."

He looked so happy. How would he feel about her if he realized she had intended to kill him? She depressed the "decline call" button, turned off the phone, and rose to her feet, kicking off her skirt, the last item of her clothing.

"I need a shower," she told him with a twinkle in her eye as she sauntered, naked to the bathroom. His cock demonstrated its appreciation of her body with a salute, and with a lick of her lips, she showed her appreciation of *his* appreciation. The urge had passed, at least for now, and he seemed oblivious to the danger. "Well," she called as she disappeared into the bathroom. "Are you coming, or what?"

****

"What was that?" yelped Terry as he shot up from the bed.

"Just the alarm clock, silly," Susie told him with a giggle. "It's time to go back to work."

He lay back down with a sigh. "I was having a great dream. I dreamed we had three kids. Two girls and a boy. I've never felt so happy."

Susie's heart flip-flopped in her chest. He wanted a family with her? She traced the contours of his washboard stomach with the tips of her fingers and felt the gooseflesh rise under his skin.

"That tickles."

She studied his eyes. Kind eyes. If eyes were truly the windows to the soul, he would make a wonderful father. The weekend they'd shared, naked in her bed, had chased away any doubts. He was the one. The man of her dreams. The man she loved.

"I've had my shower," she told him. "I'll make the coffee. Get cracking or we'll be late. After asking David to change my shift back so I could work with you, I'd hate to make him regret it."

He grumbled all the way to the bathroom, even more so when he commented on her choice of attire.

"Slacks? You normally wear a skirt to work."

She frowned her confusion. They were her best gray slacks, topped off with a long-sleeved, pale-pink silk blouse. "You don't like?"

He screwed up his nose, shaking his head as he told her, "Covering too much skin. I want to be able to touch you." His mouth curled into a grin as he continued, "It'll take longer to get you out of those pants during our lunch break."

"What am I going to do with you, Terry Palmer?"

His response took her by surprise. "Marry me."

"Is this a joke?" She leaned against the doorframe for support as he moved toward her in all his naked glory.

"I've never been more serious." His expression spoke volumes. His eyes promised love and tenderness. When he got down on one knee and took her left hand, she almost cried.

"We hardly know each other," she protested, despite her longing to accept his proposal. "How do you know I'm the right girl for you?"

"I knew you were the one the minute I first laid eyes on you. You could barely make eye contact with me but my heart recognized you. Loved you." He held her hand to his heart, his hand to hers. "What does *your* heart tell you?"

"My heart's beating so hard I can barely breathe," she whispered. "It's been that way since you walked into my life." She blinked, trying to control the tears burning behind her eyes. "I've never known a man as kind and loving as you. Yes, Terry. The answer is yes. I want to spend the rest of my life with you."

He shot to his feet so fast he almost slammed his head into her chin. She was thankful her quick reflexes saved them both. His kiss drove away any doubts.

"I haven't bought a ring," he apologized, as they came up for air. "I'd planned a romantic dinner. A proper proposal, but I couldn't wait a moment longer. The dream was so vivid, so real. I don't want to spend another day without you. I want to start making babies." He winked his left eye. "Or at least practicing."

She crinkled her nose and wiggled her index finger. "You are a naughty man." Shrugging her shoulders, she added, "I don't need a ring. Knowing that you want to marry me is enough."

"Sorry, but this is not up for negotiation." He gave her nose a kiss and headed for the shower. "After work, I'll take you shopping for a ring." He blew a kiss and disappeared into the bathroom, leaving her alone with her thoughts.

"Mrs. Terry Palmer," she said aloud. "I like the sound of that." But a lingering desire threatened to bring their perfect world crashing down.

Chapter Fifteen

Susie could hardly contain her excitement as she typed up the new cases on her computer. *Your happiness isn't at their expense,* she told herself as a pang of guilt reminded her that the clients in her reports were suffering. Besides, David's agency would do all they could to help these people. Surely she too was entitled to a little joy? She checked the time on the wall clock. Terry would be back soon and take her ring shopping. Butterflies took flight in her tummy. They hadn't talked dates yet, but she suspected he didn't want a long engagement and that was fine with her. A small wedding would be enough. The Corels and maybe—

"Where's Palmer?"

She jumped in her seat, sending her empty coffee mug crashing to the floor.

"Why do you insist on startling me?" she asked as she picked up the pieces of broken ceramic with her right hand, placing them in her left palm. As she rose to her feet, she forced herself to look into Christoff's eyes. Big mistake. As frightening as they'd been when they were ice-blue and cold, they now blazed red as he stared down at her left hand and the blood pooling in her palm.

Dropping the shards, she edged backward, her movements slow despite the temptation to run. *You'd never make it*, she warned herself.

"I won't hurt you, little one," he told her, although his expression warned the opposite. "Think of yourself as a slice of chocolate cake. I would love a taste but I can resist the temptation." He turned away. "I would, however, appreciate it if you cleaned yourself up. I've not eaten today and I've always enjoyed dessert."

There was no need to tell her twice. She rushed to the bathroom, slamming and locking the door behind her as she wondered if she should press the alarm on her watch. Was she in danger? He'd had every chance to bite her, kill her. And yet, he'd been a gentleman. Cold, yes, but not cruel. Maybe there was good in him after all?

Once she had cleaned up and bandaged the wound, she returned to the office to find Christoff had company. Anna looked concerned, even agitated.

"What's wrong?" Susie asked when Anna suddenly grabbed her hands.

"I need you to stay calm," Anna told her. Something in her tone warned Susie that this would be a big ask. "Terry's missing. David hasn't been able to contact him telepathically and he isn't answering his phone."

"I don't understand." Susie leaned back against the desk as her world began to spin. "Why do you think he's missing? Maybe he forgot to charge his phone. Maybe he—"

"What she's trying to say is that if David can't contact him through their telepathic link, he's probably unconscious."

"Nice one, Christoff," Anna growled through clenched teeth. "I'm sorry, Susie, but he's right. We believe Terry is in danger."

"No!" Susie backed away, shaking her head. "Say it isn't true."

"I wish I could." Anna reached out to touch her but stopped. "Don't answer that."

"Don't answer wha—"

The phone responded to her question.

"Listen to me, Susie, and do as I say," Anna told her. "Put the phone on speaker as you pick up. I've had a premonition. The caller is going to say things to confuse you. Fight it. Do you understand me?"

Christoff frowned. His expression somewhere between anger and confusion. Aware of Anna's psychic abilities, Susie nodded and did as instructed.

"Corel Agency. Susie speaking. How may I help you?"

A deep, familiar voice answered. "I've been calling you for days," he told her. "I've left numerous messages on your phone. Why didn't you return my calls?"

She mouthed, "It's okay," to Anna and raised her finger to turn off the speaker, but Anna shook her head. With a shrug, she answered. "I'm sorry, Beau. I turned off my phone and forgot to switch it back on. Is everything okay?"

"No. Everything is not okay. I must talk to you," he told her. "You must listen to me."

"I really don't have time for this." She was wary that Christoff moved steadily closer. His eyebrows knit and his mouth tightened into a hard, straight line. She tried to ignore his expression and the hair raising on the back of her neck as she told Beau, "We're in the middle of an emergency at the moment."

"You *will* listen to me," his voice commanded. "You will *listen* and do as I tell you. Do you understand?"

Something in his tone controlled her words. "I understand."

"Palmer is an evil man. He pretends to be what he is not. You must destroy him before he harms others. Tell me you will destroy him."

Unbidden, her head nodded. "I will destroy him."

"Enough!" Christoff's voice rang in her ears as the phone disintegrated beneath his fist. She tried to shake the fogginess from her brain. Something felt wrong. Anger boiled inside her. Hate. Her own hand balled into a fist. *Must destroy Terry*. Anna grabbed her by the shoulders, shaking her.

"Fight it, Susie. It's all a lie."

"We have to find him. He must be stopped." *A gun. Where would David keep a gun?*

"Terry is not evil. You know that." Anna held her by the shoulders, shaking her. Reasoning with her.

"Terry figured out that Beau had some sort of psychic control over you. He went to confront him. He's trying to save you."

"Save me?" What was Anna talking about?

"Yes, Susie. Save you from going down the same path as our clients."

"I don't ... what's happening, Anna?"

"You're being compelled to harm Terry. He figured out that the same thing must have happened to the other victims. You must fight it."

"I'm trying," Susie sobbed. "It's just so strong." She covered her face with her hands as she wailed, "I love Terry, but sometimes I hate him so much I want to strangle him."

"That's called marriage," Christoff informed her in a tone that gave her no indication of whether or not he was joking.

Anna spun around to him. "Will you shut up! You're not helping."

"Actually." Susie snorted. "He is." She offered him a half-smile. "I didn't know you were such a funny guy, Christoff."

Christoff shrugged. His right eyebrow raised and the side of his mouth curled as he said, "Funny? I was just stating the obvious."

Despite his objection, she noticed a twinkle in his eye.

Anna drew back her shoulders and closed her eyes. "There's more than mind control here." Her eyes snapped open. "Empty your pockets, Susie."

Susie placed her right hand into her skirt pocket. Her fingers touched velvet but she withdrew her empty hand and showed Anna an open palm.

Anna shook her head. "Give me the pouch!"

"There's nothing in my pocket," Susie objected as the urge to find Terry grew stronger. Heat radiated from her fingertips, rising through her body as her blood carried the anger to her heart. *Terry must die.*

"You must give me the pouch," Anna pleaded. "It's augmenting the hex."

"I can't," she argued. "He won't let me." Tears welled behind her eyes. *Damn you, Beau. Damn you to hell.*

"If you don't hand it over, I'll be forced to take it from you."

She tried to run, but a wall of muscle blocked her path. Strong hands grabbed her arms and held her firm.

"Let. Me. Go."

Christoff disregarded her order, his expression a mixture of amusement and annoyance as he turned his attention to Anna. "What should I do with this one? Anna? What's the matter?"

"All hell has broken loose," she told them as her face turned a whiter shade of pale. "That apocalypse we feared is happening. It's happening now."

"Zombies?"

"No, Susie. Living, breathing humans. Your friend Beau has been a busy boy. He must have called every patient in your group therapy class and then some. The police are getting calls from terrified family members all over town. They won't understand. People are going to die. Innocent people, like yourself. Derrick and the others are doing their best to control the situation, but it may not be enough. I must do what I can to help them."

Christoff released his grip on Susie's shoulders. "Then we must hurry."

"I need you here," Anna told him, motioning to Susie with a tilt of her head. "Don't let her leave the office. Promise me."

"I'm not a babysitter." He snarled, looking from Anna back to Susie.

"Derrick's in trouble," she told him as she made her way to the door. "He's my husband and he's outnumbered."

"So. That's never stopped him before. He's a strong man. A killer."

Anna shook her head. "You don't understand, Christoff. He's fighting humans. Humans under the influence of hallucinogenic drugs and hexes."

The huge vampire shrugged. "Then killing them should be easy."

"We don't kill humans. Especially those who are unable to think for themselves."

Christoff rolled his eyes and sighed. "Fine. Go assist your husband. I will ensure this little one does not kill her lover."

"Thank you." Anna turned her attention back to Susie. She placed her palms on her friend's cheeks and stared into her eyes. "Fight this. Terry needs you to stay strong." Then, she was gone.

Terry needs me? A flicker of awareness broke through the confusion clouding her thoughts. *Terry needs me.* But the shadow returned, and with it, Beau's last command. *Must kill Terry.*

Christoff walked her over to the settee and forced her down. "Sit!"

"You can't keep me here," she protested. "I must go to him. I have a job to do."

He crossed his arms over his chest and frowned. "As do I."

As intimidating as he was, she couldn't let him keep her from her task, but how could she escape? Suddenly, she knew what she must do. "I need to use the ladies room."

"Be quick," he told her as he followed her to the office en suite. "I'll be waiting by the door."

She hurried into the small bathroom, locking the door behind her before searching the vanity drawers. *Yes!* With her weapon in hand, she threw open the door and drove it into her jailer's chest.

He staggered back a few feet, bellowing, and trying to pull the bundle of wooden cuticle sticks from his left pectoral. As she tried to escape, he caught her by the hair and dragged her toward him. She reached for the empty coffee mug left on the Terry's desk and smashed it into his temple. The porcelain shattered but he barely reacted until he noticed the re-opened wound on her hand.

"Stop this foolishness!" he roared, his blue eyes now as red as the blood trickling from her palm.

Except she couldn't stop. Couldn't ignore the commands ringing in her ears. Despite her fear, her torment, she fought on. Her fists pounded his chest, driving the makeshift stake further toward his heart. He bellowed and his eyes flamed as he pulled out the offending object. Fangs sprung from his gums. "Enough!"

"I can't stop," she cried as she fought to drive the murderous, conflicting thoughts from her head. As much as the voices drove her to kill Terry, her heart fought the desire to harm him. *Terry needs me.*

"Help me, Christoff. Please. Help. Me."

Her hand slipped inside her pocket and Christoff snarled. "I advise against another attack."

She shook her head and held out the red, velvet pouch. "I don't know how it works or where it came from, but it feeds my hate. Take it, please take it away from me before it completely controls me. Before it turns me into—"

"Gollum?"

I never expected that. "You've seen *The Lord of the Rings* movies?"

"Phff. I've read Tolkien." He took the hex bag from her hand. "I've seen this type of magic before. It was made for you, and you alone. I will destroy it before it does any more harm."

"He's still in my head," she cried, holding her hands over her ears in the hope that she could block out the homicidal urges. *Please, God. Don't let me hurt Terry.* "He's so strong."

Reaching out with both hands, she flexed her fingers, her biceps twitching, her arms shaking. As her body rocked, the muscles in her jaw clenched to the point of pain. Christoff seized her. His strong hands held her by the wrists. Blood pooled in her palms and, in that instant, she made a decision.

"Exchange blood with me."

Christoff dropped her hands and backed away, scowling as if her request had repulsed him. "Do you understand what you're asking?"

She nodded. "Can you stop the voices in my head?" Voices that called to her, even as she asked her question. Murderous voices commanding her to do awful things.

"Little one"—the corner of his mouth curled into a smirk but the color of his eyes remained blood red as he informed her—"if I do what you request. *I* will become the voices in your head."

Part of her wasn't ready. A big part. He terrified her but more distressing was the thought that she might actually hurt Terry. She didn't wait for a response.

"Do it!" She thrust her palm at him, her feet already itching to leave. "Do it before I change my mind."

As he accepted her hand, she steadied herself for a frenzied, painful attack. Memories of her previous experience with the rogue vampires flooded back, turning the contents of her stomach. His tenderness surprised her. This huge, aggressive-looking vampire tenderly lapped the blood from her palm, never once attempting to bite into her flesh. Once he'd taken enough, he tore a small hole in his own wrist and held it to her mouth.

"Close your eyes. I've been told it's better if you don't look."

She did as he instructed, tasting the coppery tang of his blood on her tongue. Feeling his life force in her cells. Hearing his voice in her head telling her that she was going to be all right now. The fogginess dissipated. She expected to hear his instructions, his commands. Instead, she heard her own. *Go save Terry.*

****

Terry opened his eyes and cursed the pain that felt like a bullet to his brain. "Son of a bitch." He tried to sit up but found that his hands were tied behind his back. His feet secured with heavy ropes. With difficulty, he managed to push himself into a sitting position to lean against a cold, damp wall. As his eyes adjusted to dull light, he took in his surroundings. "What the hell?"

The brick walls of the small room were lined with shelves full of jars and strange objects. He squinted, trying to make sense of the contents of the assorted jars.

Fuck! Is that a human fetus? Beside it, a large cobra lay coiled, its head positioned to strike. He remained as still as he could manage. Watching. Waiting. For the longest time he studied it until, at last, he realized it was dead. A taxidermy work of art. He let out a sigh of relief, knowing he stood little chance against a poisonous snake. People he could manage. Snakes ... not so much. Especially tied up and defenseless. How the hell had he gotten here anyway? He wracked his throbbing brain for an answer. *Last thing I remember is going to Dr. Dubois's office. Someone must have got the jump on me.* It seemed likely that the dampness behind his head was a result of a bleeding wound. Probably had a concussion too, judging by the pain and memory loss. Experience warned him of the danger a concussion posed. *Must stay awake.*

The more he tried to find clues by scrutinizing the contents of the shelves, the more convinced he became. *This guy is truly fucked up.* He struggled against his bindings. The rope burned his skin, but he had to escape. No way was he going to become the contents of one of those jars. He wanted his eyes exactly where they were, in his head, not on display in a psycho's dingy, lair. A wave of panic washed over him. Bile rose in his esophagus. *What if I never see Susie again?* He'd been in tight situations before yet none had affected him so viscerally. *Can't do this to her. Can't put her through another trauma.*

Using his buttocks to maneuver, he wiggled toward a low shelf and began to slam his feet into the brick wall. The shelf trembled against the force of the blow, shaking the heavy jars. *This could work.* He kicked again and again, building momentum. Watching the jars wobble precariously until... Smash! Two jars hit the concrete floor, shattering the glass, spilling the contents on the ground. He gagged as the pungent smell of decaying flesh permeated the small room. He tried to ignore the squishy sensation between his fingers as he sifted through the congealed muck for a sizeable shard of glass, grateful that he wasn't able to see whatever it was coating his hands.

With a large shard jammed against the brick wall behind him, he began to force the rope binding his wrists in a downward motion against the glass. Occasionally, he felt the sharp sting of tearing flesh as the rope slipped, but he continued until the job was done. With his hands now free, he grabbed his makeshift knife and cut through his ankle bindings before reaching for the waistband of his jeans. *Dammit! Where's my gun?* Using the wall to support his wobbly legs, he rose to his feet. *All right, Palmer. Now what?* His head swam. Pain radiated, not only from his head wound, but from his entire body. *How long did I lay on this cold floor?* Checking his watch, he cursed the beautiful timepiece that David had gifted him. The hands told him that it was two o'clock, but unlike his old digital watch, it gave no indication of whether it was night or day. He'd left for the doctor's office at eight in the morning. Surely he hadn't been imprisoned for only four hours? No. His cramped and aching muscles disagreed with that theory. More likely sixteen hours. *Shit!* Susie must be beside herself with worry. With a heave, he forced himself off the wall. *Now, where's that door?*

****

Susie paced the office floor, wringing her hands and grumbling obscenities under her breath.

"You can call me anything you wish," Christoff told her from his position on the couch. "I can't let you go."

She stopped in front of him, pleading, "I have to

find him. It's after midnight. He could be dead by now."

"I have my orders."

She screwed up her face at him. *Now, he decides to listen to instructions.* A smile spread across her face. "I thought you were your own man. I didn't think you'd take orders from anyone, especially a female."

He appeared confused. His eyebrows furrowed. Deep creases formed between his eyes.

"You can't fool me, little one." He wiggled his index finger. "You'll stay here until Anna returns."

"Damn it, Christoff. Who knows how long it will be before Anna comes back." She kicked the coffee table, sending magazines flying in all directions. "If anything happens to Terry … so help me I'll—"

Christoff crossed his arms across his chest and put his big feet on the coffee table. "You'll do what?"

Before she could finish her threat, his pocket began to vibrate. She held her breath as he answered his phone.

"Berg."

"Who is it? Is it Anna? Have they found him?"

He held his hand palm out to silence her.

"Yes. I know the place. Who? Yes. She's no longer under the enthrallment. I'll explain later." He placed the phone back in his pocket and rose to leave. "I must go."

"Hold your horses." She grabbed him by the jacket sleeve. He looked from her hand to her face and frowned. She immediately released him. "Tell me what's happened."

"David has located Palmer through their telepathic link. He's unable to attempt a rescue so he's given me the coordinates."

"What are we waiting for?" She grabbed her bag from the desk and tried to push past him.

He held out his arm, blocking her path. "You, will stay here."

"Not on your life, buster."

"Technically, I'm—"

"Yeah, yeah, undead. I know. Regardless, I'm going with you."

Christoff raised his hands and shrugged. "You'd better not get in my way."

She poked out her tongue and screwed up her nose as she challenged, "Or what?"

"Or I'll treat you to a song or two while you try to sleep," he warned her telepathically. *"I have several hundred in my repertoire."*

Now I know how Terry feels when David talks in his head. She sighed as she locked the office door behind her. As she turned toward the hall, a thought suddenly occurred to her. A thought that took her breath away. A thought that sent a shiver of panic down her spine. Dark outside. *I'm going out in the middle of the night with a vampire. A vampire who even terrifies other vampires.* She blew out a long breath and remembered all the times Terry had told her how brave he believed she was. He'd be proud of her. Proud of the courage he'd known it took to face this challenge. If David was able to connect with him, he must still be alive. As they hurried to Christoff's car, she silently prayed he'd stay that way.

****

"Why are we stopping here?" she asked Christoff when he pulled up to the curb of the red brick building.

"This is where David told me we'd find Palmer." He studied her face. "Why have you gone pale? Are you ill?"

"This is my doctor's office," she informed him. "She also holds the clinic here."

Christoff glanced out of the window then back to

her. "Perhaps it would be best if you waited in the car."

The sinking feeling in the pit of her stomach warned her that she should listen to him, but her heart overruled it. Terry may be in there. "When will the others get here?"

"The others?"

"David, Anna. You know. The Corels."

"They are still occupied elsewhere," he told her, offering no explanation as he exited the car. "Your enthrallment may be over but, I fear the danger is not."

She threw open the passenger door, calling out to him as she followed. "What do you mean they're not coming? *Why* aren't they coming?"

He turned so fast, she almost collided with his chest. After a moment's pause, he sighed and grasped her shoulders.

"I know this may be hard for you to understand, little one. We are in the middle of a war. David and the others are in the fight of their lives. You heard Anna. Their hands are tied. Against a vampire, they would win easily, but their enemies are humans. Their efforts to save these humans may bring about their own demise. Each of the Corels are in different locations trying to protect the families from their own loved ones. Loved ones affected by hallucinogenic drugs and Voodoo magic."

"Can't the police help?"

Christoff lowered his chin, looking up at her with his piercing blue eyes. "The police would not understand. They would be forced to kill the very people David and his family are trying to save."

Susie nodded. "I think I understand." She stared at the door of the building. "Why would Terry have been taken here?"

"Do you remember the phone call at the office earlier?" he asked.

With a shrug, she told him, "Not really. Only that afterward, I really wanted to hurt Terry." She grimaced as she added, "And you. Sorry about that."

He looked down at his torn shirt and the blood stain close to his heart. "That was my favorite shirt."

"I'll buy you a new one," she offered with an awkward grin.

After checking the deserted street for witnesses, he broke the front door open with little more than a push and ushered her inside. "That man, Beau, was the caller. He told you to kill Palmer."

"Why would he do that?" she gasped. "It doesn't make any sense."

"It makes perfect sense," he argued as they stepped into the elevator. When the doors closed, he told her. "Although I hadn't heard his name in years, I recognized the voice on the phone. You see, Beau and I have a history. His real name is Buford. Buford Moroux."

She leaned back against the wall of the lift and shook her head in disbelief. "How did you know him?"

"I was sent to destroy him for his use of the dark arts. He was, and it appears that he still is, a bokor."

She watched the light above the door flash three and continue upward. "A what?"

"Bokor. Voodoo priest."

The elevator stopped with a thump.

"This is where the meetings are held," Susie told Christoff. "Do you think Beau ... I mean Buford will be holding Terry here?"

He held his finger to his mouth and disappeared. In a wink of an eye, he'd returned. "The fourth floor is empty. Wait inside the meeting room while I search the other floors."

Before she could protest, he'd vanished. She trudged to the empty room and waited by one of the large, floor-to-ceiling windows to gaze down below to the street. Not a soul ventured outside. Why would they? Most people would be safe and sound, asleep in their cozy beds at this time of the morning. She rubbed at the gooseflesh on her arms. The temperature had dropped. There was a definite chill in the air, especially in this big, empty room. She tried to remember if Terry had been wearing warm clothes when he left the office. What did Buford plan to do to him? Why must she wait here when Terry needed her?

"Susie?"

She turned toward the familiar voice. "Dr. Dubois. What are you doing here?"

The doctor frowned. "I could ask you the same question."

"I'm … waiting for a friend." *Who is taking his sweet time coming back.*

"You shouldn't be here," the doctor told her. "This building is restricted."

"I'm sorry." Susie made her way toward the doctor, wondering if she should mention Buford. "Look, Dr. Dubois. There's something I think you should know about Beau."

The doctor reached into her pocket. "I can't discuss other patients with you. You know that, Susie."

"But what if he's doing something illegal? Surely that overrules doctor-patient confidentiality?" *What is she holding in her pocket?*

"All right, you have my attention. What is it you want to tell me about Buford?"

"Have you heard of a bokor?"

The doctor's smile sickened her to her stomach and something jelled. She hadn't mentioned Beau's real name, but somehow the doctor had known all along. She *knew* what he was doing. Probably helped him. Terror gripped her by the throat and squeezed, robbing her of the scream that strained beneath its grip. As Dr. Dubois lifted her hand from her pocket, Susie glimpsed the handle of a gun and rushed the doctor. They grappled for control of the weapon. The gun fired past Susie's head, narrowly missing her. She ignored the ringing in her ears as she fought for her life, trying to stop her attacker from getting a better shot.

They wrestled. The weapon fell to the floor and they both grabbed for it, the doctor reaching it first. She raised the gun by the barrel and swung the handle at Susie's head. Susie raised her left arm to protect her face and felt the impact on her wrist, the watch taking the brunt of the attack. Pain radiated from what she instinctively knew was a broken wrist. Before she had time to react, a second strike hit her temple, knocking her to the ground.

She blinked away the blood that trickled down from her temple in time to see Dr. Dubois raise the weapon and aim it at her face. As she closed her eyes and waited for the bullet that would end her life, she heard a male voice.

"What are you doing, Charlotte?"

"Stay out of this, Buford. This doesn't concern you."

Susie opened her eyes, stunned to hear the hate in her doctor's voice. What had she done to deserve this? As if he'd heard her unspoken question, Beau asked, "Why are you doing this? It wasn't in our plan."

Our plan? What *were* they planning? How did it involve her?

Beau casually approached the not-so-good doctor and reached for the weapon. She snatched her hand away. "You can't talk me out of this."

He shook his head, tapping his temple with his

forefinger. "Think, Charlotte. Use that clever mind of yours. We need her alive in order for the plan to work."

"You mean *you* need her."

She turned her attention to him, giving Susie the opportunity to reach for her watch to call for help. With a sigh, she realized the little heart-shaped alarm had been crushed. The watch was reduced to a broken frame attached to a band. The face of the timepiece shattered.

Beau's words shocked her back to the situation at hand.

"Are you jealous, lover?"

"Of her?" Charlotte spat the words, scowling in Susie's direction. "I could break that little bitch like a twig."

Excuse me? Susie's blood boiled. *We'll see who breaks who.* Unfortunately, when she tried to sit up, the pain and swelling in her wrist reminded her that she'd been handicapped and her head throbbed from the blow. Where the hell was Christoff? Why was he taking so long?

"I've been busy," the voice in her head told her. *"I've found Palmer."*

She glanced around the room. *"Did I imagine his voice? Is it the concussion?"*

"Why do you ask so many questions?" he complained. *"I warned you that we'd have a telepathic connection."*

"Christoff?"

"Who else would it be? Wait ... I sense danger. What has happened?"

She inhaled a deep breath. *"The doctor and your friend Buford are in cahoots. I'm trapped. Terry? Is he...?"*

"He's alive. Slightly concussed, but otherwise uninjured."

"Oh, thank God." She almost cried aloud but managed to keep her expression blank. She could use this telepathic link to her advantage. *"Christoff, can you hear what I hear? If I can entice my captors to talk, will you be able to listen in?"*

"Yes, but why? I can be there almost instantly to assist you."

"No! No. If you attack them, we won't know what they're planning. We have no idea what permanent effect their drugs will have on the patients. I have a better idea."

"Fine. Wait ... Palmer is objecting to your suggestion. He demands we come to you."

"Don't let him!" A smile tried to curl her lips. She fought it down. *"Tell him I know what I'm doing. Ask him to trust me."*

She waited for an answer. *"Well?"*

"He trusts you. That is all I'm prepared to relay. I refuse to repeat the other mush. He can tell you himself later."

"You're awfully quiet."

Susie looked up to see both Beau and Charlotte staring down at her. *"Here we go,"* she told Christoff. "I've been trying to work it out. Why are you hurting your patients? What's in it for you?"

"Revenge and money," Beau answered without hesitation. "Isn't that what everyone wants?"

"Buford!" Charlotte snarled, but he ignored her protest.

"What's the harm in telling her?" He shrugged. "She'll forget everything once I compel her again." As a frown creased his brow, he asked, "Wait a minute. Why didn't you kill Palmer?"

"I couldn't find him," she told him truthfully. Then, for effect, she added, "I've searched everywhere for him. He must die."

"You won't find him here." He snorted, but his smile faded when Charlotte grimaced. "What did you do to him?"

"He turned up at the office yesterday morning, asking questions about the drugs I've been giving my patients. He wanted a list of the ingredients and their contra indicators. I pretended I was going to my outer office for a list before hitting him with a marble bookend."

"Where is he now?"

"Don't worry." She stroked her man's arm. "I have him locked up downstairs. He's not going anywhere."

Beau pushed her away. "You idiot! What if he finds the antidote?"

"Are you getting this?"

"Find out what the antidote looks like. What does it do?"

"How the hell am I going to do that?"

Before he had a chance to answer, Charlotte solved the problem.

"Don't you call me an idiot!" She pointed the gun at his chest. "No one gets to call me an idiot."

"Put the gun down, my love." He gently took the gun from her hand and placed it on the shelf behind them. "I am sorry." He stroked her cheek with the back of his finger. "We've worked hard to get to where we are. I don't want anything to go wrong now."

"I've hidden the capsules in a nondescript brown bottle behind the jar of intestines in our private room. No one will think to look there. Besides, he's tied securely." She turned to Susie. "It should be easier for her to kill him now."

Susie swallowed the lump in her throat. If

Christoff's telepathic link hadn't broken Beau's hold over her, she may have been enthralled to kill Terry.

"You're welcome. By the way, Palmer has located the bottle. We're coming to assist you."

"No. Get the antidote to David. They won't hurt me while they believe I'm under their influence."

She waited for a response. *"You are right. While I'm away, Palmer can assist you—"*

"No! Keep him away. With you gone, I may not be able to resist their compulsions. I can't risk hurting him."

"As you wish, but we'll be back soon."

Knowing that Christoff and Terry had left the building, Susie felt very much alone. Pain radiated through her head and hand and Charlotte stared daggers at her while she remained on the floor, unable to rise. *How could I have been so gullible? I trusted this woman.* She looked away, unwilling to make eye contact with the psychologist. So many broken, desperate patients had put their faith in her treatments only to be exploited. Why?

As she willed herself to her feet, she solicited more information from her captors.

"I still don't understand. Revenge on who? And how does that make you money? Are you blackmailing someone?" Her hand reached out to grab a chair for support as her legs began to shake.

Buford laughed, but his smile twisted into a sneer as he told her, "I knew that if we could create a little chaos, my old nemesis would surface. Charlotte provided me with a way of distributing my … shall we call it, Zombie formula? Once the pills had been administered, I'd call the patients and plant the suggestions to kill their families. Sure enough, Christoff Berg emerged from whatever hole he's been living in since driving me from my home."

Susie's right hand flew to her mouth. This was all

about Christoff? But how would that make Charlotte rich? She asked the question out loud. "Where does the money come into it?"

It was Charlotte's turn to smirk. "All of my patients signed over their life insurance to me. Once they killed their families and then themselves, I'd be sole beneficiary of a stack of policies. Which reminds me. I have some papers for you to sign."

Susie shook her head and turned toward Buford. "Christoff will stop you again. He'll drive you from Azure Waters just like he drove you from your last home. The Corels will help him. I will help him." She directed her next threat to Charlotte. "As for you. You won't see a cent of that money. I'll tell the police everything you've said."

"My dear Susie." Buford snaked his way over to her. "The Corels aren't going to help Berg. They're going to *kill* him."

She backed away, cradling her broken wrist. "Never. You can't compel any of them. It isn't possible."

"Don't you think I've done my research?" He growled. "The Corel brothers protect the humans in this community while our friend Christoff is a cold-blooded killer. We've made sure that there are too many people for them to deal with without someone getting hurt. He has no love for humans, but his friendship with David Corel goes way back. If David is harmed, there's no telling what Christoff will do, and then the rest of the family will be forced to exterminate him. It's their law. I'm sure he'll take at least one of them down with him. Either way, it's a win-win situation for me."

"And a few more monsters off the street," Charlotte added.

"Monsters?" If she'd learned anything from her time with Anna and her family, it was that they were the kindest people she'd met. "*You* are the monsters. I hope they lock you up and throw away the key."

"I've had enough of this small talk." Buford reached out and grabbed her arm. "It's time for you to finish off Palmer."

She struggled to free herself as he dragged her toward the door. "Why Terry? What does he have to do with any of this?"

"Oh, why don't you just shut up," Charlotte screamed in her face. "I'm sick of all the questions."

"No, I think she deserves to know the part she'll be playing in Berg's demise." Buford stopped beside the door, pinning Susie against the wooden frame. "You see, my dear Susie. You are our extra *insurance* that Christoff goes rogue."

She narrowed her eyes and opened her mouth to question him, but he silenced her with the answer.

"After you kill Palmer, Christoff will be forced to punish you. I doubt very much that the Corels will allow him to hurt their little pet. You will be the last straw. The final nail in his coffin."

Slap! Her uninjured palm connected with his cheek. "You bastard!"

His laugh still rang in her ears as his accomplice hustled her out of the room.

****

Of all the occasions he'd been forced to bide his time, this had to be the toughest. He'd recognized their voices, all three of them, and understood why Susie had delayed them with questions. Damn, she'd make a fine detective. Each answer revealed a crucial detail about the plot to, not only kill Christoff, but to annihilate whole families for the sole purpose of exacting revenge. No, not just revenge. Greed played a large part. Greed always played a part.

They'd stopped at the door and he'd almost lost it when Beau pinned her against the frame, but he'd talked himself down. *Wait. Not yet.* For a moment, he'd worried that she'd seen him hiding outside the room. Would she accidentally give him away? Apparently, her attention remained focused on the big man because her eyes didn't leave his face, even when she struck him. *Good girl.* His heart almost burst with pride. She had guts, his fiancée.

Susie exited first, followed by the doctor, and then the target of his anger. Terry lunged, knocking Beau face first to the ground and almost toppling Susie. For a split second, Dr. Dubois froze, staring down at him as he wrestled the big guy's hands behind his back. She reached into the pocket of her jacket and cursed before running back inside the room with Susie hot on her heels. *That's my girl.*

He turned to the sound of a crash as something hard hit the floor. Beau took the opportunity to flip over, forcing him onto his side. They wrestled, his opponent managing to take a few cheap shots with his fists. His eye began to swell, blurring his vision. *That's gunna leave a bruise.* He returned the favor, scoring a couple of solid punches to the big man's nose. Blood gushed down his chin and pooled on the collar of his shirt, but rather than slow him down, it seemed to spur him on. His hands wrapped around Terry's neck and squeezed. Terry could feel the blood rushing to his cheeks. The pressure building behind his eyes. His consciousness fading.

Was that a scream? He fought the darkness that had begun to wash over him. *Must fight. Fight for Susie.* He slammed his right arm across his chest, connecting with Beau's elbow, breaking the grip on his neck before using the momentum of the strike to bring his elbow back and into Beau's temple, not once, but three times. Saliva dribbled from his opponent's mouth. His eyes rolled back into his head just before he lost consciousness. A gunshot rang out, followed by another scream. *Susie!*

****

When Charlotte reached for the gun that she'd left on the shelf by the door, Susie lunged for her. The momentum took them both down. The gun slipped from her hand and slid across the wooden floor. Charlotte stretched out her arm, her fingertips almost touching the handle.

Not again! Susie's temple still ached from the last assault. No way would she give the doctor another chance to control the gun. She grabbed a handful of the other woman's hair and tugged, pulling her head back briefly before slamming her face-first into the floor. Simultaneously, both women screamed. Susie's wrist throbbed from the exertion. Charlotte's scream probably in response to the wound to her forehead, but there was to be no relief for either because Susie continued to pound the doctor's face until she ceased in her attempt to grab the gun.

"Susie!"

She turned her head to the voice, closed her eyes, and sighed. "I thought she was going to kill you." Tears burned behind her eyes. What if she hadn't been able to stop Charlotte from reaching the gun?

"I thought she *had* killed *you*." Terry smiled down at her. "I think you can get off her now. You've beaten her unconscious."

"What about Beau?"

"Same." He stepped around the women and grabbed his gun. "I think they'll both sleep all the way to jail."

She lifted the unconscious woman's head. "Oh. I guess I got a bit carried away, but when I thought of what she tried to make me do…" She allowed Charlotte's head to hit the ground. "I should have killed her."

Strong hands gripped her shoulders and lifted her to her feet. He wrapped his arms around her and she fell apart, sobbing into his chest.

Warm lips kissed her forehead. "No. You're not like them. You fought the compulsion to do harm."

She shook her head. "Only after I convinced Christoff to take my blood. If he hadn't helped me, I don't know what I would have done." She raised her head to stare into his emerald eyes. *What if I'd killed the only man I've ever loved?* "I was weak, Terry. I can't stand the person I've become. Cowardly, pathetic, frightened of everything—"

"Frightened? Are you kidding me?" He held her at arm's length, his face beaming with pride. "After all you've been through, you asked a vampire to take your blood and you didn't do it for yourself, you did it to save me."

"I'm not sure you'd call that brave." She shrugged, but the realization of what she'd done suddenly hit home. *I actually asked a vampire to control me?*

His laughed reverberated through his hands, shaking her shoulders. "Not just any vampire either. Christoff even frightens *me* and I've heard the other vampires give him a wide berth because of his reputation. Not brave? You picked the biggest, meanest son of a bit—"

"If you finish that sentence," the voice from the door told informed him, "you'll discover how I came to earn that reputation."

"Christoff. Did you get the antidote to David in time? Are they all okay?"

"Yes, little one. The situation is under control." He looked down at the woman on the floor. "You seem to have taken care of the perpetrators. I found her lover in the hall and took him to the police station while you had your little chat. The officers expect a report from you, Palmer. Shall I escort this one too?"

"She may need a visit to the hospital first," Susie told him before reaching up with her good hand to touch her own forehead. "I may join her."

"I can take away your injuries." Christoff's expression softened. His voice reflected the concern on his face as he sent her a telepathic message. *"I will not harm you."*

"I appreciate your offer, but, I'm sure it's nothing."

He opened his mouth to protest. She silenced him using their mental link. *"I'd hate to shatter his faith in me. He thinks I'm brave, but I'm not sure I'm up to going through a blood exchange twice in one day."*

"Your wrist, little one. You do realize it's broken?"

She nodded. *"Yes, I know. Maybe tomorrow I'll call on you to help me. Tonight ... I'll rely on an emergency doctor and painkillers."*

Terry squinted as his gaze shifted from Susie to Christoff. "What am I missing here?"

"You have a fine woman, Palmer," Christoff told him as he scooped the unconscious doctor from the floor and threw her over his shoulder. "Take her to the hospital. I'll inform the station that you'll be in tomorrow."

"Wait!" Susie called to him before rushing him with open arms. She reached up on tip-toes, cupped his face in her hands, and kissed his cheek. "Thank you."

His head dipped in a subtle nod, but she detected the hint of a smile on his lips before he disappeared.

Terry came up behind her, wrapped his arms around her, and whispered into her ear, "Should I be jealous?"

Heat radiated from his body and her own body relaxed against his chest. She closed her eyes. *Almost lost this*. "Stop talking and hold me," she told him as tears streamed down her cheeks. "Just hold me."

Chapter Sixteen

"This is so surreal," Susie whispered into Terry's ear as she sat, curled up in his lap on one of the large, leather sofas in the living room of the Corel residence. Despite an entire coven of vampires surrounding them, she felt completely at ease. Funnier still, she almost pitied the strangers who had been called to debrief the events of the last few weeks. Vampires who'd bravely rushed to answer the call to arms, yet cowered under the watchful eye of the man she now called friend. Christoff stood leaning against a doorframe, his impassive expression visibly disturbing the other guests. Susie stifled a grin, suspecting it was his intention to have that effect.

"Friends." David raised his voice above the crowd. "Thank you all for coming to our assistance. I'm pleased to announce that Buford Moroux has been deported back to Haiti, along with his partner. The antidote has been distributed and all the victims are recovering nicely. We couldn't have accomplished this without your help." He lifted his wine glass in salute. "Here's to the return of tranquility and to our continuing friendship."

A chorus of cheers rang out, along with the clinking of glasses. All except one.

"Why aren't you toasting, Christoff?" Susie asked, cradling the fresh cast on her wrist. *I don't like that look on his face.* "What is it that you're not telling us?"

He shifted away from the door, his actions stirring movement of half the room as they jumped in their seats. The other half reacted with gasps. But not Susie. She'd come to understand him and the wall he'd erected to discourage conversation. *Big, tough, vampires*, she scoffed. If only they knew how thoughtful he could be.

"Moroux and his lover were indeed a threat to this small town." He hesitated and turned towards Susie. "Their complete lack of compassion for the doctor's patients and the families of those patients proved how dangerous the situation could have become, had it not been for the bravery of our young friends." He motioned toward the only humans in the room. Susie smiled as Terry's arms hugged her closer.

He whispered in her ear, "See, even Lurch thinks you're brave."

"Shh."

"But the bokor was only a taste of what's to come. The danger that drew me to this country has not yet revealed itself."

Terry lunged forward in his seat, almost toppling Susie from her perch on his lap. He caught her before she fell, whispering an apology before addressing Christoff's revelation.

"You're telling us that there's something else out there? Something worse than a Voodoo priest dealing in black magic?"

"I am."

"Care to elaborate?"

Susie felt a slight shove. Then Christoff's voice came through clear in her mind. *"You have overcome much in the last few weeks, little one. Are you sure you want to push your limits?"*

She nodded her answer. He acknowledged the slight movement of her head, mirroring her action. He turned his attention to the group, specifically the brothers Corel.

"Years ago, I vanquished a powerful mage who, like Moroux, sought to control and wreak havoc. Unlike the bokor, this sorcerer was narcissistic and a high-functioning sociopath who did not depend on spells to convince people to do his bidding. Soon, his greed for power became insatiable and he turned to the dark arts, finally selling his soul to a demon before I expedited the transaction. Somehow, his spirit has resurfaced."

Susie couldn't help but notice Meaghan reach for David's arm and raise her eyes to him. The realization hit home. *Damn. If vampires feared demons, what hope do we humans have?* Terry must have come to the same conclusion.

"Fuck me."

All eyes turned to him but only Meaghan commented, "I think we all share Terry's sentiments. We've recently dealt with a demon and I'm not keen on repeating the experience. What can we expect from one who's in cahoots with a mage?"

"Danger. Danger and mayhem." He frowned before continuing. "I believe that this, not the events of the last few weeks, is the apocalypse Anna saw in her visions."

"Don't sugarcoat it." Terry squeezed Susie tighter. She could feel his heart pounding against her back. Although he tried to retain an air of confidence with his nonchalant words, she knew how much this revelation had shaken him. He'd told her about his encounter with a demon. How he hadn't believed in their existence until Meaghan had been offered up as a sacrifice. The experience almost killed Terry and forced David to turn Meaghan into a vampire in order to save her life. No wonder they both looked as pale as sheets, Meaghan more so than usual.

A barrage of questions shot at Christoff from all directions. Apparently, Meaghan and Terry weren't the only ones troubled by the news. David stilled the anxious voices with a wave of his hands. "All right, Berg. Tell us the plan of action. What should we do?"

"Stay out of my way." He turned and headed toward the foyer, David hot on his heels.

"Wait! You can't do this alone."

Without slowing his pace, Christoff called over his shoulder, "I can and I will."

****

"Well, that was delightful." Terry opened the door to his car but Susie shook her head.

"Let's go for a walk in the garden before we go home."

He tilted his head to one side, squinting as he said, "You do realize it's two in the morning?" The last time he'd taken her out at night, she'd freaked out. Had she even realized the time?

"It's a beautiful night … I mean, morning. Let's enjoy the flowers. While we were inside, I noticed that the balcony fairy lights were on. I haven't been in the garden at night before. Please, Terry. I'm sure they won't mind."

Wrapping his jacket around her shoulders, he led her around to the back of the Corel mansion. "Not that I'm complaining about spending time with my beautiful woman in a romantic setting, but, it's pretty dark out and—"

"And the house is full of vampires?"

He nodded, expecting the realization to send her hightailing it back to the car. "Wouldn't you prefer to go home?"

"I have news for you, Terry Palmer."

She reached up and touched his face with the palm of her good hand. His heart fluttered in his chest at the warmth of her skin. The warmth of the gesture. *So, this is what love feels like?*

The patio fairy lights reflected in her beautiful eyes as she told him, "Home is wherever you are."

As he closed his eyes for a moment, he prayed that when he reopened them, she'd still be there. In his life. In his arms. *Don't let this be only a beautiful dream.*

"I don't deserve you," he told her as he cupped her hand to his face. He drew her hand to his lips and kissed each knuckle. "But if you'll give me the chance, I'll spend the rest of my life trying to be more worthy of you."

"Are you kidding?" She shook her head and laughed. "When we first met, I could barely look you in the eye, do you remember?"

He responded with a shrug and a smile. Of course he remembered the timid little mouse in David's office, hiding behind Derek. The most beautiful woman he'd ever seen. "You'd just been through an ordeal. It wasn't your fault."

"I know that … now. It took me a long time to understand that there were still good, gentle people in the world. People like you."

"I don't know many people who'd describe me as gentle." He chuckled.

"Maybe not to your face."

Her half-smile and wink sent a surge of blood to his crotch, leaving his head groggy from the blood loss. *Is this real? Is it possible she loves me as much as I love her?*

"If I've had anything to do with your recovery, I'm pleased to have contributed, but you've done all the hard yards yourself, Susie. Look how far you've come. You faced a Voodoo priest and wrestled a woman for a gun. You not only allowed, but you actually persuaded a vampire to take control of your mind. Even now, do you realize this is the first time you've purposely ventured out after dark since your abduction?"

"I have you to thank for that," she told him. "I was only able to do all of those things because I couldn't risk losing you. You've given me the strength to face my fears, to take back the night."

Overcome with emotion, he pulled her against his chest, cradling her head in his palm as he hugged her. "Until I met you, I've never really known fear, never cared what happened to me. When you suddenly turned on me, I thought my life was over. I lost the strength to go on. You're not the only one who feared the night. Without you, my nights seemed endless, dark and lonely. I don't know how I would have survived another night without you in my arms."

Dampness soaked his shirt. He felt the muffled sob reverberate through his chest, igniting every cell in his body, acknowledging her acceptance of his love. She lifted her chin. The green in her hazel eyes blazed against the mocha background, and he instantly recognized the significance. He'd seen that expression many times in the recent weeks. Come-to-bed eyes. His cock jumped in appreciation.

"Take me home," she told him with a sly smile as she tilted her head toward the bulge in his jeans. "We have a lot of catching up to do."

"Why wait until we get home?" Surely he could find a secluded part of the garden. He needed her. Now.

She shook her head and took off running. "Last one to the car is a rotten egg."

He followed her. Not in the physical sense, but with his eyes. Followed the curve of her bottom in those snug jeans. Followed the bounce of her breasts as she sprinted down the path. Followed the glow of her golden locks as the wind lifted the curls.

He took his time walking back to the car, enjoying

the view, planning their future in his mind. But he'd learned from previous mistakes. *No rushing her*. She'd been through so much in her short life. More than most could bear and she'd handled it with class. *What a woman*. He wanted her, body and soul, but more than that, he wanted marriage, kids, the whole shebang.

She reached the car and turned, frowning. "I thought you were in a hurry?"

"I am," he told her as he threaded his fingers through her hair, cupping the back of her head as he drew her in for a kiss. He'd have those things he wanted so badly, in time. For now, all he wanted was Susie. In his bed, in his life, forever in his heart.

The End

www.annieharlandcreek.com

ANNIE HARLAND CREEK

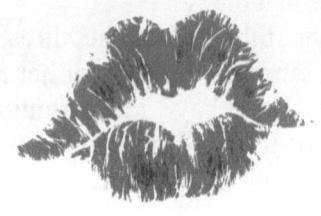

EVERNIGHT PUBLISHING ®

www.evernightpublishing.com